BEFORE THE SINK OVERFLOWS

(AND OTHER WARNING SIGNS OF HOPE)

ALL STORIES BY

DREW G. ROSEN

ISBN: 979-8-9995390-1-4

DEDICATION

To those we walk beside—whether for a step or a lifetime.

And to Kenji, who taught me how much can be said without a single word.

INTRO

In this debut collection, a retired wrestling champion finds grace in the game of pickleball, a father uncovers the courage to face his past in the moments of a physical therapy session, and a student grapples with a difficult writing assignment. From the anonymous kindness of a cell phone salesman to the unshakable awareness of a crossing guard, these stories reveal the hidden lives of people just trying to make it through the day.

Before the Sink Overflows is a moving portrait of the small moments, daily routines, and unseen labors that define us all—a reminder that some of the deepest truths are found not in grand gestures, but in the spaces between unexpected change and the search for purpose.

EPIGRAPH

"The miracle is not to walk on water. The miracle is to walk on the green earth, dwelling deeply in the present moment and feeling truly alive."

—Thich Nhat Hanh

TABLE OF CONTENTS

BEFORE THE SINK OVERFLOWS

That morning, I had the kind of premonition you can't prove but can't shake—a foreboding feeling tuned just beyond clarity. Still, I stuck to the routine: wheat bran floating in oat milk, tossing yesterday's semolina crumbs in the general direction of the birds who never said thank you.

My wife texted: *Hair iron still plugged in?*

She asks every Tuesday and most Thursdays. It has never been true.

I replied with the usual emojis: house, fire, gun.

Saxson, the rat terrier with a God-given limp and a vet-given prescription, took his constitutional dump on the corner of Larch and Maple. He looked smug about it.

Still, the feeling gnawed at my gut.

Something was circling.

My watch read 7:42 a.m. Mandy would be rolling out of her rumpled dorm room bed, zipping up her nor'easter canvas bag while sipping scorched black coffee from a sunflower-yellow Yeti as she walked to Ruddley Hall for American History 101.

Last night, she'd called, her voice quieter than usual, pausing mid-sentence before pivoting to some term from class. I pressed the phone between my ear and shoulder, transferring damp laundry to the dryer, losing another ankle sock to the ether. The lint trap was clogged with pink elastic and fleece, and I cleaned it with two fingers and a practiced grimace.

The screen door upstairs slammed with such drama that the kitchen flinched.

Trevor, my seventeen-year-old, was back from his morning run.

I climbed the basement stairs, shaking damp lint from my fingers, and stuck out my fist for a bump, knowing that anything other than the slightest acknowledgment of his existence could spawn a heated exchange. His knuckles grazed mine as he reached for the ancient blender and kicked off his sneakers. He dropped in five frozen strawberries, a scoop of whey protein, some ice cubes, and a splash of what I hoped was unexpired almond milk. The electric growl of the blender's motor filled the room.

I watched Trevor, wearing one sock, chug his smoothie with preposterous urgency. He wiped his mouth with the back of his hand and looked up at me. I knew the look; it's the same look his mother gave me when there was something to say that I was not going to like.

My mind scanned the possibilities: Will this cost me time, money, or pride?

"Uncle Ryan called," he said, setting his empty glass in the sink without rinsing it. "He's coming by soon."

The sick feeling in my stomach crystallized into something sharp and defined.

The last time my brother and I were face-to-face was at Dad's funeral. He showed up late, reeking of bourbon, and tried to pocket Grandpa Mike's old watch from the casket display. When I called him out, he swung at me—left me with a black eye and a cracked pair of Ray-Bans. His departure was less exit than escape.

Trevor turned on the TV in the living room. Some singers I had never heard of were accepting an award I didn't recognize.

I went to the sink to rinse the residue from the dirty glass. As the sponge reached the depths of the bottom, I swept the strawberry achenes up in a swirling motion.

"He just wants to talk," Trevor mumbled from the other room.

I stepped into the threshold between kitchen and living room, water still running behind me like a secondary thought.

"You've *spoken* to him?" I asked, unable to hide my disappointment.

"Yeah, what's the big deal?" Trevor shrugged, not quite meeting my eyes. "It was just once. He said it was important."

"Trev, this is the same guy who missed your championship game. Made Mandy cry on Easter. For God's sake, he nearly let Saxson out last time he was here! And let's not forget how he circled like a vulture when Grandpa Mike died."

Trevor put down his phone and muted the TV with a dramatic flourish.

"You gotta chill, Dad," Trevor said, his voice softer now. "Maybe he wants to apologize. Or maybe something's wrong.

"He sent me a text last month—about that old skateboard he gave me for my tenth birthday. Said he missed those days. I don't know...it was weird, but kind of nice.

"I mean, he used to be around more, right? Before things got...whatever they got. He was the one who taught me how to ollie. Took me to that skate park in Wexford, remember? That stuff meant something to me back then."

"Tell me exactly what he said," I demanded.

The water kept running, and for once, Trevor looked at me. A real look—not the drive-by glances we'd been trading for years.

He shifted in his seat, thumbed his phone, but didn't look at it. I could see the fight in him—something between defense and compassion, like he wasn't sure if protecting Ryan was the right call or just the easier one.

I leaned against the doorway, arms crossed. Waiting.

"I don't remember the exact words," Trevor finally said. "He just said he needed to come by to talk. Something about Mandy. He sounded...I don't know. Different. Maybe nervous?"

That scared me more than anything.

The faucet still ran in the other room. The sound had become a kind of static, like a faulty radio station playing behind our conversation. I imagined the sink filling, inch by inch, until it spilled over the porcelain lip and onto the kitchen floor, soaking through the tiles, down into the basement, eventually rotting the foundation of the house.

I pushed off the doorframe and stepped back into the kitchen. Turned the water off with a firm twist. The sudden silence was jarring.

That's when we heard it. The crunch of tires on gravel. Trevor and I looked at each other.

We didn't move. Just listened as the past pulled into the driveway, idling outside the house like it owned the place.

The water wasn't running anymore, but I still heard it.

I dried my hands on the dish towel, took a breath, and walked to the door.

HOLD THE JALAPEÑOS: AN INTERVIEW WITH GLADYS SANDS

S etting: A slightly worn but clean hotel breakfast area, just after the morning rush. The smell of coffee and lingering bacon hangs in the air. GLADYS is wiping down a table, takes a moment to lean against her cart.

Intro: The steel industry has been in a state of collapse for decades. Yet Pittsburgh, perpetually on the heels of a cultural revolution and a "turnaround," continues to grow. Gladys Sands has crossed the Monongahela River over the Hot Metal Bridge more times than she can count. But the trip downtown lets her make the most of her job at the Admirable, a long-standing hotel in Allegheny County. She says the constant work allows her to make better sense of a crazy world.

Q: How long have you worked here?
A: Wow. I've been with the Dutch sisters for twenty-seven years. (Shakes her head, a small, tired smile.)

Look at that, wow. The last ten at this Admirable location on Fairfax. It's been good. I remember when the hotel had trouble filling rooms. Right after that whole virus and vaccine thing. But not anymore. It seems like the theater and the flea market down on Drellers Street keeps people coming in. And I'm just happy to do my part. You know, they let me take home the extra biscuits, too. That's a blessing. Lord knows Esther and Ben—they are my godparents—but they live with me now, they love those biscuits. I remember one Christmas, Jack, he's the manager, good man, he was up front. He saw me, said, "Gladys, you take all these sausage patties, these muffins." (Chuckles softly.) Santa came early that year, yes he did.

When that virus came, did you know I didn't miss one day of work. Not one shift. Even when the bus was not running, I cobbled together rides. Walked farther than I care to remember. Wore out those black sneakers. But I made my way through that revolving door—every day.

Q: If you could put up one rule on the wall, just for you, what would it say?

A: Oh, that's easy. "Take what you're gonna eat, but eat what you take." It's the jalapeños mostly. Little green fellas. Folks pile 'em up like they're stacks of coins, you know? Then they eat one. Maybe two, if they're feeling brave. Rest of 'em? Pushed aside. Buried under a mound of salsa, some pile of potato. And those spuds don't cut themselves, you know. That's Clarence. He's in the back. Good people, Clarence.

People had more mind about them years ago. You might not remember, but there was a time when folks would take what they could eat, maybe come back for seconds if they were still hungry. But now it's like these fancy phones have people in a trance where their eyes are bigger than their stomachs. No one thinks about the people that could fill their bellies with powdered eggs and day-old rolls.

Last week I had a lady, all dressed up, jam a five-dollar bill in my hand. "I can tell you take pride," she said. I mean, why wouldn't I? People got places to go and if I can keep the tables clear and the dishes fresh, then I'm playing my small part in their vacation or business trip. We get pilots, too. Airport's not far. They're quiet, the pilots. But they like their fruit. And they got manners. "Please," "thank you." You notice that. Things change, no doubt. But syrup, well, syrup still sticks, don't it?

Q: What's something about this job that nobody sees—but matters?

A: It's the oatmeal. (Laughs.) People think it makes itself. But that big pot? You gotta pour the boiling water just right so it doesn't clump, or burn your skin. When I first started, there were weeks where my hands would blister just from the steam. Then you gotta stir it for twelve, thirteen minutes—steady, or it gets that icky skin on top. You try doing that once or twice a morning, hundreds of times. Your elbow flares. Once me and Pearl Gee, she was my dishwashing partner for years before she passed over, may God bless her soul, we got to talking about how we could convince both Missus Dutch to skip the oatmeal entirely, and just get more cold cereal choices. But they told our manager that even if people load up on sugars and fat, the vat of oatmeal makes them feel like they got a choice. And that choice to indulge while on vacation could be the difference of another stay in the future, or a choice to just stay home and do nothing at all. Now I can tell just by sound if it's ready. Oatmeal don't lie. It's thick or it's not.

Q: Ever think about quitting? Hanging it up?

A: (Leans in a little, voice drops conspiratorially.) You said this interview is private, right? Like there's no way my bosses will know it's me? (Interviewer assures Gladys that her identity will be protected.) Good. 'Cause this is overall a good place to work. No one gets mad if I need to go see my doctor. And when you get to be where I am on the arc of life, there ain't no more reinventions waiting to be had. This is it, you know. Beats running register at one of them big-box stores or something like that. People gotta start their day the right way. (Pauses, a faraway look.) I'm sorry, what was it you asked? (A soft chuckle.) Oh, yeah. Quitting. You asked if I thought about quitting? Honey, probably five times an hour, every morning, for twenty-seven years. (A wider, more genuine laugh now.) Wouldn't be a job if you didn't want to quit it, would it? But I still show up. That door spins, and I go through it.

JOINT VENTURES

I destroyed my shoulder by sleeping on it funny.

Not sleeping on it funny every night, but one single, solitary hour of sleep on the living room couch after I passed out eating $42 of takeout from New Dragon East and watching *How It's Made: Aluminum Foil*.

That's all it took.

And now my imaginary pitching career is over before it started. But at thirty-eight, I don't think anyone is looking for a five-foot, ten-inch single guy who could barely touch 57 mph on a radar gun.

56.8 mph to be exact.

At least according to the red neon sign standing at the Guess the Speed game at the Holy Spirit Carnival last summer.

It was the most humbling $5 I've ever spent.

The good news is that Dr. Felixson, the orthopedist who stood before me in Air Jordan 4s, three inches taller and thirteen years younger than me, declared that the X-rays were inconclusive and the best path forward would be a round of potent anti-inflammatories and to see a physical therapist, which conveniently, they had in the same building.

"How often do I have to go?" I asked.

"Well, you don't 'have to' do anything," Dr. Felixson said. "But if you want your full range of motion reestablished, I'd recommend two to three times a week for about six weeks. Again, just my professional recommendation."

I thanked him for the advice and folded the script into my sweatpants pocket.

There's no way I'd make the eighteen-minute drive several times a week, it was hard enough getting the energy up for this visit. So, I set out to find a PT closer to home. As luck would have it, the old Tutor Teachers a few blocks away recently reopened as a physical therapy center.

I made an appointment online; there was a two-week wait.

As the days went on, I was 75 percent certain my shoulder was better. Not because of the drugs—I never filled the prescription—but maybe due to the healing powers of Father Time. I considered ghosting my first appointment at Joint Ventures Physical Therapy but figured it couldn't hurt to see if I could get my range of motion back to 100 percent. For that matter, it couldn't hurt to leave the house again either.

A girl with skin that glowed like polished amber and red-framed glasses met me at the front desk with a sheepish smile. After a scan of my driver's license, health insurance card, and credit card, she pushed across a clip-board jammed with papers.

"All of these?" I asked.

"Yes, please," she replied without ever looking back up at me.

I scanned the freshly painted waiting room with its bare white walls and obnoxiously bright LED lights, and took a seat in the middle of a long row of identical blue plastic chairs against the storefront window. I wondered how many people a day had their shoulders heated and iced like blanched broccoli.

After filling out my name for the eighth time, I encountered a series of questions that made me lol.

If your problem made sounds when you moved, what would the person next to you hear?

If your injury/condition were a houseguest, what annoying habits would it have?

Well, these intake forms just took an odd turn—from annoying paperwork to fiction writing class.

I decided that my shoulder would sound like a raw steak being torn apart and that, as a houseguest, it was always there, following me from room to room, lurking.

Nineteen pages later, the therapist now had my life story, a $30 co-pay, and emergency contact information three times over.

As I sat back down in the waiting room chair, the receptionist, whom I would later know as Crystal, glanced up.

"Some of those questions are ridiculous, right? The houseguest one?"

She paused.

"The doctor will see you now," she announced.

I entered a room that was sparse: black foam floor, mirrors aplenty, a few simple benches pushed toward the middle of the room, a rack of colored dumbbells, and a tall young man organizing stretch bands of all sizes hanging from hooks.

"Hi. Dr. Chuck Mendoza," the man in the gray hoodie said as he approached me with his arm extended. "Call me Dr. Chuck."

"Robert Fredricks," I replied. "Call me Rob."

"So, what brings you in today, Bobby?" Dr. Chuck asked as we walked onto the training floor. "Do you prefer Bob? Bobby?"

"Rob is fine," I replied.

I wasn't annoyed that he was asking my name preference right after I gave him my name preference. It was the fact that I had just written a novel about my arm issue at his office's request, even turned it into a sirloin roommate, yet here we were, back at the beginning.

"My left shoulder," I said. "It's just been off."

"Ah, the heart attack arm," Dr. Chuck said as he turned to address a tall young man who was now sitting on a large red yoga ball to his left. "That's the one that always brings them in. Right, Malik?"

The kid forced a small grin, exposing tiny teeth, and nodded. He seemed to be getting accustomed to working with Dr. Chuck, who might have been looking for a sidekick to his comedy show as opposed to a PT assistant.

"Didn't really cross my mind," I started to reply before getting cut off by Dr. Chuck.

"C'mon. Just looking at the gray in your beard and that slouch in your back, it's gotta have crossed your mind at some point," the doctor said.

And with this, he was standing behind me, pushing down on my shoulders while guiding me to sit on the cushioned bench behind me. Sensing the tenseness in my body as he felt around my upper back and arms, Dr. Chuck shifted gears.

"So, what type of work do you do, Rob?" he asked.

"I'm in accounting at Six Atlas Bank." I replied.

"Ah, so hunched over a computer all day. I knew as soon as I saw you walk in. Didn't I say that, Malik? Desk guy, incoming."

"I do my best to move around," I said. "But sometimes the day just gets the best of me."

"I hear you, brother." Dr. Chuck said, getting too comfortable too quickly. "See this?" he asked, motioning toward our reflections. "These rounded shoulders mean you have some serious tech neck."

Then, softer: "But don't worry. You're not the first to sit in that chair thinking they're falling apart. And you won't be the last." He paused dramatically. "Don't worry, dear Rob, I've got the cure."

I wanted to hate this guy, I really did. But even as the large digital clock on the wall mocked me, trudging along like it had nowhere better to be, I couldn't shake the sense that maybe—just maybe—he wasn't entirely full of shit.

"You been sleeping okay?" he asked, quieter now. "Stress can sneak into the muscles, especially around the shoulders."

"Uh, yeah. Mostly." I said, caught off guard.

"Well, I find people are usually here for more than one thing," he said, kneading the edge of my shoulder blade with surprising gentleness. "Whatever that might be, we'll uncover it and work on that, too."

He felt up and down my arm, stopping at random intervals to apply pressure with his thumb.

"Does this hurt?"

"Not too bad."

"This?"

"A little tender," I admitted when he reached the side of my elbow.

The doctor motioned to Malik, who walked across the room to a large chest that smoked when he opened it. When he returned, he wrapped my elbow in a large towel, asking if it was too tight. I told him it wasn't.

"We're gonna let that heat up a bit," the doctor said as he walked to the front of the room to greet an incoming patient.

"How's the knee, George?" he asked.

An older man in blue jeans two sizes too large started telling Dr. Chuck that he had missed most of his at-home exercises since his sister was in the hospital with food poisoning after a trip to the DR.

I used this conversation as my severance point and consciously decided to tune out the squeaky pulleys and the pedaling bikes as my elbow warmed. With my eyes closed, I took a few deep breaths in through my nose and exhaled out of my mouth. My mind flashed to Alyson—probably under the Eiffel Tower by now.

We used to talk about that trip. Never the right time, never enough money. Until she found a way. I always blamed her for leaving, but if I'm honest, I'd been drifting, too, just in the same spot, pretending I wasn't lost.

"Meditating over there?" bellowed Dr. Chuck. "Don't drift away too far. I'll be back with you in a few minutes."

I didn't respond because I knew the PT was only speaking to hear himself talk.

A few more deep breaths and I imagined Malik choking his boss, biceps bulging, wide smile, never uttering a word. Just walking away after taking in the silent room for a quick beat while the doctor lay motionless, and then getting on the bus to go home.

The thought warmed my heart. It also made me realize that my elbow felt like a two-alarm fire.

"Excuse me," I said to Malik, who was seemingly standing by just for this type of incident.

"Too hot?" he asked.

"Yeah, it's burning a bit," I said.

Malik undid the heat dressing as Dr. Chuck rolled over on a backless stool.

"How are we doing over here? All good in the Garden of Zen and Fire?" he kidded. He then explained that he would do a deep tissue massage and that very little was expected of me.

"Just sit back and let Dr. Chuck do the healing," he said. I rolled my eyes.

He wiped some cream around the crook of my elbow and used his thumbs to glide down the inside of my arm, reversing course at the base of my wrist and working back up to the ball of my shoulder. The smell of sandalwood and mangoes danced under my nose.

"As I work through your muscle fibers, it's not going to be a picnic," the doctor said, breaking the thirty seconds of glorious silence. "But we're looking for 'good pain,' the kind that helps inform—"

I winced as Dr. Chuck rolled past the top left of my elbow.

"Like that!" he said, followed by an obnoxious laugh. "Now I know where to target."

"Heeeey, Florence," he said as he swung around to greet the next patient, a woman in her sixties with one crutch, tired eyes, and wispy blond hair.

"Look, Malik, no hands," she said as she balanced on one leg, making everyone incredibly nervous.

"All right, Flo, simmer down before you get stuck with me for another eight weeks," Dr. Chuck said.

Meanwhile, my face was scrunched from the pain near my upper shoulder as the doctor continued to rub my arm, but, with the focus on Frantic Flo, no one noticed. It got so bad that I desperately let out an audible cue by sucking through my teeth.

"Ah, we have another hot spot," the doctor said as he swung around on the stool to face me. His thumbs remained pressed on the tender area. "That's pain radiating from the subscapularis, a small muscle hidden beneath the shoulder blade."

Frankly, I was getting more and more irritated. I wanted to let the doctor know that I was not here for an anatomy lesson, and I didn't need the recipe for healing; I just needed to feel better.

"Hey, I'll be right back with you," the doctor said as he got up to talk to George, the old man with the bad knee and a beige camouflage hat pulled down so low that the brim covered his eyes.

Malik trailed the doctor, offering some quiet and sound advice as he passed me. "When there's a hot spot of pain, do your best to exhale."

I wondered why the best advice was not coming from the doctor. Dr. Chuck seemed more concerned with chatting up each patient, making everyone feel seen, rather than working on each person's individual problem.

That's not an awful thing. In fact, maybe it's somewhat noble in today's fleeting world.

But I'm sure the old man with the bad knee and the lady with one crutch want to get back to their old selves as badly as this guy wants his shoulder fixed, well, as much as a thirty-eight-year-old shoulder can be fixed.

Dr. Chuck returned, rubbing my arm a few more times before having me stand before him to conduct a few exercises.

"They're only three pounds each," he said, referring to the green dumbbells he handed me. "But you're gonna feel it in the morning."

He then turned to Malik, who was always within a few feet of Dr. Chuck, and told him to run me through the I, Y progression. And then end with the lacrosse game.

Malik led me through the exercises, which were simple enough. His silence made me wonder if my form was perfect (unlikely), or if he really was *that* quiet.

The last exercise he had me perform was a plank with my outstretched arms leaning on a round wooden balance board that rocked back and forth. Holding it steady was hard enough. But then Malik pointed to the hole in the center and told me to catch the rubber ball he dropped on the board.

I literally felt like I was circling a drain.

"Having fun yet?" Dr. Chuck asked as he walked past me. The squeak of his obnoxiously high pink Hoka running shoes annoyed me more and more with each step.

"We're all set," Malik announced.

"Excellent! So, what do you think?" the doctor asked, as he stood in front of me, shoulders squared like an offensive lineman.

"Not too bad," I replied. My tone as monotone as the words were generic.

"See Crystal at the front to make your next appointment," he said. "And be sure to do your homework."

With that, he handed me two black-and-white printouts with the exercises we worked on during the day's session.

Arms shaking, elbow throbbing, I made my way back to the reception area, passing a teenage girl in a volleyball uniform who was met with a big high-five from Dr. Chuck.

"Bye, Bobby. See you next time," he said.

I stood awkwardly at the front desk for several moments as Crystal navigated a call about wrong insurance information. I surveyed her desk. A tin of spearmint Altoids. Two fake sunflowers sitting in a red ceramic mug. A small photo of a small dog with long silky hair. Maybe a Maltese?

I eyed the thick black hair running over Crystal's shoulders and landing on a black flannel shirt that led to black leggings that terminated in a pair of chunky black boots. While I was trying to lump this girl into a bucket defined by a Spotify playlist, her call ended, and she looked up at me with a smile.

Oooof. The smile took her from *the receptionist* to the kind of girl you are making wedding plans with.

"You have serious patience," I said, referring to her handling of the phone call—and having Dr. Chuck as a boss.

"Just doing my job," she said. "So, let's see here. Looks like you were approved by your doctor for six weeks, three times a week. Should we go and schedule that out?"

"All of it?" I squeaked, unable to hide the surprise in my voice.

"We do find that works best for all parties," she said from some memorized script.

My calendar used to be an issue. But now it's mostly just me, me, and more me. "Let's start with next week," I replied.

And with that, I was on the books for Monday, Wednesday, and Friday.

"Please don't forget that we have a strict twenty-four-hour cancellation policy. No exceptions," she warned.

"Got it," I said.

"Have a nice day," she said.

"You as well," I replied.

"And Robert," she added, as I opened the door, "do the homework, it always helps."

I nodded, fairly certain that I would never see Pinball Chuck or Silent Malik ever again. But after a weekend of doing the shoulder exercises and feeling no worse than I did when I started, I begrudgingly found myself parallel parking in the rain on a Monday morning outside of Joint Ventures PT.

"What a way to start the week," bellowed Dr. Chuck as he held the front door open for me. I rushed out of the car and thanked him for holding the door.

"First appointment of the day means you're stuck with just me to start. You can settle up with Crystal after our session," he said.

"Sounds good," I replied.

I followed him into the training room and placed my wet hoodie on the chair planted next to the therapy bench.

"Ya know," he said, "you're already moving better. I can tell you did the homework."

"Yup, I doubled up on Saturday, too," I said.

"Whoa. Someone wants an early release," he chided.

He took my arm and wrapped it in the heat pack, not as tight as Malik had the previous Friday.

"So, how was the weekend?" he asked as he sat next to me on the swiveling stool.

"Not bad," I said. "We had a nice dinner for my son's birthday."

"Niiiiiice. How old is he?"

"Ten, but already burping like a college freshman."

"Whoa! Slow down there! My guy just turned two months old."

"Oh, man. Congratulations. You seem well rested for having a newborn."

"Dude, he sleeps like a sixteen-year-old Labrador. Give him a bottle and he passes out."

And with that, Dr. Chuck wheeled over to a stand with a laptop and a coffee-stained Styrofoam cup.

"Ugh," he called over. "Phil canceled his ten a.m. Gotta charge him anyway."

I'm not sure why I needed this information or if the doctor was using it to reinforce the rules with me.

"That's too bad, too. He really needs some more cupping therapy if we're going to get him up and moving fully again."

"Does that pseudoscience actually work?" I asked, instantly regretting the words as they tumbled out of my mouth.

He wheeled back toward me.

"Rob, if we get a few extra minutes today, I will cup you up, and you let me know if you give a shit about the lack of evidence the scientific community requires to make something true medicine."

The words came out hot. Hotter than my elbow, which Dr. Chuck was now unwrapping.

"Forgive the language," he said. "I just get upset when people keep their minds closed to possible solutions."

"I'm open, Dr. Chuck," I said. "If there's time, let's do it."

"Hell yeah," he said, uncapping the massage lotion and getting to work on my arm. "Your arms and back will never feel better."

Being alone in the office with him, having a bit more of his focus, felt good—literally. I felt the muscle fibers in my damaged arm paying attention. It hurt, but in that weird way that reminds you something is alive in there.

Kind of how it felt to talk to people again.

"Good morning, doctor," Crystal said softly from the other end of the room.

I'm pretty sure she was wearing the same outfit from Friday. Seeing her standing, though, was a different experience. I couldn't put my finger on it. She was a few inches shorter and a few years older than I had first noticed, late thirties maybe, and there was something oddly attractive about her.

"Would you mind cueing up the Silver Playlist?" Dr. Chuck asked her.

A few seconds later, "Under the Boardwalk" started to blare from the Amazon Echo in the corner of the room.

"Silver because it's all oldies?" I asked.

"A healthy diet of the Platters, the Coasters, the Drifters, and *the* Elvis. All for Ms. Beasley. She'll be here any minute and the familiar music helps put her at ease."

And with that, Malik materialized, seemingly out of thin air.

"Good morning, Leek," Dr. Chuck said.

"Hey, Doc. Hey, Robert. Good morning, Crystal," Malik said. He was trailed by the older man from Friday, who was back for more therapy.

"How's the knee?" Dr. Chuck asked George as we were reaching the end of my arm massage. I knew because the motions were getting faster and deeper.

"Well, you know, my brother-in-law needed my help with the boat this weekend, so I wasn't able to get to my homework," George said.

"Bad boy, George H. Quinn," Dr. Chuck said.

"Actually, my middle initial is A," George corrected.

"I made it up, George. All in an attempt to scold you for missing your at-home work *again*. You really need to keep up with it if you want an honorable discharge. So, what does the A stand for?"

"Anthony," George said.

"What's your middle name, Leek?" asked Dr. Chuck.

"Malik Amari Carter," he replied.

"Yes! That makes you MAC!" the doctor replied, way too happy to have a new nickname for his assistant.

Dr. Chuck turned to me.

"And you, Robert 'not Bobby' Fredricks?"

"Well, there's a story behind it," I said.

"This is gonna be good," Dr. Chuck said, smacking his lips. But first, he yelled out toward the reception area.

"What's your middle name, Crystal?" She peered her head around the wall.

"Don't have one," she said.

"Weird," Dr. Chuck said. "We'll come back to that one. But you're up, Rob."

"Well, it's Fredrick," I said.

I surveyed the room, finding perplexed looks everywhere I scanned. Even Crystal had her forehead crinkled and eyebrow raised as she processed the ridiculousness that my name is Robert Fredrick Fredricks.

After some laughter from Dr. Chuck, he said, "Well, it could be worse."

"How?" I asked.

"Your first name could be Fred."

Everyone chuckled. Meanwhile, Dr. Chuck was already greeting Ms. Beasley at reception as "Yakety Yak" played out of the speaker.

Malik took me through the same exercises as last week as George pedaled away on a recumbent bike.

"How long have you worked here?" I asked Malik, breaking the silence between exercises.

"I'm in the final year of my DPT program," he said. "But I've worked on and off with Dr. Chuck for almost ten years."

"Wow! My kid's ten, so I know that's a long time," I said. "He splits time with his mom. We're figuring it out."

The words were received as awkwardly as they fumbled out of my mouth.

"Anything else?" Malik asked Dr. Chuck as he pointed at me.

The doctor was sitting with Ms. Beasley at the far end of the room, and from what I could tell, he was patiently explaining a certain stretch to her, possibly for the sixtieth time.

"Yes!" he said. "Let's add clocks."

Malik handed me a green resistance band, which I stretched out chest-high with my wrists. With my hands against the wall, I started at twelve o'clock and worked my way in a circle, struggling a bit when I hit the nine and three positions.

"Three more times," Malik instructed.

By the third round, my arms were trembling like thin branches in a storm.

"All set," Malik said.

As I headed toward reception and passed George on the bike, I said, "Nice work."

He responded with a head nod.

"Don't forget the homework," Dr. Chuck said, looking up briefly as he had Ms. Beasley's left leg over his left shoulder.

I stood at the front desk while Crystal finished something on the computer. Her screen had a blackout shield, but I imagined she was updating some kind of patient record. "The Great Pretender" by the Platters played, and Crystal stated that I had a $30 co-pay. I handed her my debit card, and the processing felt like forever.

"Please put in your pin," she said, holding up the keypad.

I pressed the buttons too lightly and then I pressed too hard as the poor girl did her best to balance the terminal in her hand.

"Do you need your receipt?" she asked.

"No thanks," I said.

"Okay, let's look at the calendar here. Looks like you're good through this week but I would recommend scheduling out the rest of your appointments to make sure we have availability."

Back to Scripted Crystal.

"Can we do Monday, Wednesday, and Friday at the same time next week?"

I didn't love committing like this, but Crystal had a job to do, and my shoulder *was* feeling a touch better.

"You're in the books," Crystal said. "Have a nice day."

"Thanks, you, too," I replied.

I wanted to say something else. Ask if that was her dog in the photo. If she liked the Silver playlist oldies as much as Ms. Beasley did. Hell, what she thought of Chuck's endless schtick. But I drew nothing but blanks.

As I opened the door to leave, I turned back and said, "I'll do my homework," like some dorky seventh grader who had never talked to a girl in his life and found a way to reveal his love of wizards, labyrinths, and math in one fell swoop. I'm not sure if she replied because I never turned back around.

But as I got in the car, I opened my calendar and added reminders for next week's sessions. That felt...new.

Most weeks lately had been stitched together from leftover takeout containers and low-stakes Netflix binges.

But this week, Ben was coming over Friday after school, my every-other-weekend kid. He was ten, whip-smart, obsessed with weird facts about space and the probability of alternate dimensions. We usually did pizza and video games.

Maybe this weekend we'd do something else. Something a little more...active.

Wednesday's appointment came, and I found myself standing outside of a locked office. The lights weren't on, so I assumed Dr. Chuck and the staff were running late.

The late-April air had a hint of sweet warmth and my face turned toward the sun like a plant hungry for chlorophyll. I'm not the praying type but I do embrace hope, and my hope was that this spring and summer would be easier than last year, after the fallout from Alyson's transgressions, which split our lives in half.

George, with the bum knee, walked up behind me.

"Door locked?" he askcd.

"Yup," I replied, physically giving the door three small tugs.

"Easy there, cowboy," George said. "Don't want that shoulder to regress."

"Very true," I said, surprised that he knew what ailed me. "How's the knee coming along?"

"Good days and bad days. But at eighty-two, I'm just happy to be around and moving with all my original parts."

I was floored.

"Holy cow. Eighty-two?! That's amazing, George. I would have never guessed."

"You want the secret?" he asked.

Before I could answer, Crystal barged between us from behind, rattling a ring of keys.

"I'm so sorry," she said. "We are all running late this morning."

She sounded like she was fighting back tears, but with a deluge of hair in her face, it was hard to tell.

"Hey, we're all late sometimes," I said, trying to put her at ease.

"My schedule is wide open until...forever," joked George.

The front door swung open, keys bouncing aggressively against the glass. Crystal's black tumbler hit the white tile floor, blasting green tea fifteen feet in every direction. She attempted to place her large knit bag on the reception chair, but the contents spilled everywhere.

"I can't," she said, running to the bathroom to compose herself.

Instinctively, I knelt behind the desk to pick up Crystal's belongings, placing them back in the bag one at a time. I came across a small sketchbook with Japanese lettering. I was dying to know what was inside.

There was a prescription bottle with a single pill.

There was a worn copy of *The Let Them Theory* by Mel Robbins, whose podcast I listened to regularly.

There were not two but three phone charging cords.

And a pack of Big Red gum.

"You okay down there?" asked George.

I looked up at him and his face wore general concern.

"Yes, yes. Didn't realize a woman could fit so many things in her bag," I said, hoping to defer any attention away from me.

"You a married man, Rob?" asked George.

"I was," I said.

"Oh. Sorry," George replied.

"Don't be. I'm sorry that my shitty life predicament just walked us into an awkward conversation," I said. I felt that familiar red burn in my cheeks; the breath caught high in my chest, but I continued. "Was married for fourteen years. I thought we were happy. She thought we were floating apart. So, she decided to sleep with the UPS guy."

"She's not the first," George supported.

"Yeah, I'm sure those guys get it all the time from married women. Must be the little brown shorts," I said.

"No, I mean she's not the first to have made dumb choices instead of just communicating openly and honestly," George said. "I know because I made that dumb choice. Twice. It was a long time ago. Decades." George paused, a dull glint in his eye as he remembered the moments his life went sideways. "We were high school sweethearts. And then I got a little too cozy with my tennis coach. She was a beautiful woman. Long legs, long auburn hair, green eyes. I mean, my Maddie was pretty, too. Turns out the coach and I had a lot in common in our home lives: go home to our spouses, eat dinner, think about sex but not have it, then go to sleep, wake up the next day, and do it all over again.

"One day, we're complaining and confiding, and the next, we're kissing at center court. Anyway, when it ends, it ends ugly. Let's just say, I didn't play much tennis after that. But here's what I figured out. You can never win if you're always obsessing about where your last shot went wrong. You have to reset, forgive your mistakes, *and* forgive *their* mistakes. I had to forgive myself for what I did to Maddie, but I also had to stop keeping score of her reactions. Sometimes the greatest ace you can serve up is just letting someone walk away with no hard feelings."

"Wow, George," I said, not wanting to say anything that would reveal how shaken I felt.

We stood there for a beat—just two men in the waiting room looking to be fixed. George looked at me like he hadn't said anything extraordinary.

I'd spent so much time painting Alyson as the villain that I'd never really considered the second act—the one where you forgive someone just so you can start being yourself again.

"Thanks for sharing that," I finally said. My voice came out thinner than I expected.

George nodded once, like that was all he needed.

Crystal reemerged, clearly having cried but having pulled herself back together in time for work: high ponytail, freshly glossed lips, and a touch of mascara to hide her rough morning. She forced a smile as she made her way around the reception desk.

Dr. Chuck barged through the front door with Malik right behind him.

"I am so sorry, crazy traffic on the turnpike," the doctor said as he went straight to the workout floor. "Let's go, guys," he said to George and me. "There's no time like the present to start healing."

On the workout floor, Malik set both of us up with heat. Shoulder for me, knee for George. This would give the office staff ten minutes to get it together after the late start.

A single guitar strummed through the speaker. I knew the song.

A *warning sign*
I missed the good part, then I realised
I started lookin' and the bubble burst
I started lookin' for excuses

"Coldplay, nice," I said.

"Is it?" Dr. Chuck replied. "Not my playlist, it must be Crystal's."

I closed my eyes. Finally, I thought. A deeper dive into the intriguing receptionist.

The songs from Crystal's playlist kept coming.

Snow Patrol, "Run."

The Fray, "Over My Head."

The Doves, but I couldn't place the song.

Words, they mean nothing
So you can't hurt me
I said words, they mean nothing
So you can't stop me

Man, this girl sounds lost, holding on to some serious early 2000s trauma that could only be aided by plaintive piano chords and beautifully broken lyrics. It was strange how familiar this place had become in just under a week. The same faces, albeit a new patient or two, the same routines. The past Monday, Wednesday, and Friday, I found myself in this room, arm wrapped in heat, watching George pedal on his bike, listening to Ms. Beasley hum along to oldies. I was even starting to anticipate Dr. Chuck's jokes, occasionally beating him to the punch line in my head, which both annoyed and satisfied me.

The sound of the peeling Velcro jolted me back to reality as Dr. Chuck removed the heat wrap from my arm.

"Soooo, what's new?" he asked.

"Not much. No new injuries, so score one for the Middle Ages," I said.

"How old are you?"

"Thirty-eight."

"So, you're tapping out at seventy-six? I'm going to give you some advice, and you may not like it, but it's not like you're going anywhere," he said with a cocky closed-mouth grin. "Stop with the middle-aged babble, that's nothing but an excuse for the unwilling. The only thing you need to concern yourself with is that right now, at this very moment, you're the youngest you will ever be in this lifetime."

Wow. Genuine insight from Dr. Chuck. I was surprised. But also realized, reluctantly, that the man had a point.

Dipping his fingers into the brown tub of massage cream, he continued.

"People are so afraid of growing older," he said, working the cream into my shoulder with vigor. "They forget that aging is a privilege. Your body isn't betraying you; it's just asking for different conversations." He paused, then added more softly, "And not just the body. Everything worth keeping needs maintenance—shoulders, relationships, hope. Most folks give up at the first sign of wear."

I sat with that for a moment, wondering if this was real therapy all along with Dr. Chuck purposely distracting his patients with bluster to make space for the hard truths, slipping them in with patients hardly noticing.

"Anyways," he said moving into his massage finale. "You got time today for the cupping treatment?"

I pulled my phone out, pretending to look at my calendar.

"Indeed, I do."

Malik was with Florence, guiding her through a series of gentle bends against the mirror wall.

Dr. Chuck briefly disappeared and reemerged with a silver attaché case that looked like it could have held a small rocket, spy secrets, or hundreds of rare Pokémon cards.

He unlatched the case and popped it open with the excitement of a young artist showing off their new set of oil pastels. Inside, there were sixteen glass cups of various sizes, a short gray plastic hose, and a small hand pump, the kind you would use to inflate a saggy soccer ball. I'm not sure what I expected, but the cupping set seemed more rudimentary, and my face must have told the story.

"Look," Dr. Chuck said. "When you think about it, what could be more primitive than applying negative pressure to your body? But that extra blood flow to heal the damage to your muscles and fascia is going to feel great."

"Is it going to hurt?" I asked.

"That's a question for Malik," he responded, as he pointed toward the kit and pointed to Malik and made his way to greet Than, a twentysomething Vietnamese man who Dr. Chuck was helping with a cervical spine compression after a car accident. Apparently, Than had been on the last delivery of the day, bringing the Joint Ventures staff a late lunch from Magglio's Deli when he was rear-ended by a kid driving his mom's Kia Carnival. Insurance was paying for the treatment and Than's lawyer was insistent that he never miss an appointment to help with what could be a "high-six-figure settlement." At least this is what Dr. Chuck told me last week as he walked me through an exercise that had me passing a ten-pound kettlebell under my chest as I held myself up with a single arm.

Malik made his way over and started wiping a few glass cups with an alcohol wipe that he tore out of a foil pouch.

"Shirt off," he instructed.

I reluctantly pulled the black T-shirt over my head, sending locks of thick blond hair into disarray.

"Is this going to hurt?" I asked again.

"Nah. Just a little pull each time I vacuum a pod," he said.

I thought about how out there this was for me. Handing over control with minimal details was not my specialty. But in the name of pseudoscience, and a growing trust in Chuck, I figured, why not?

"It might be cold," Malik said as he placed the first cup on my upper left back. This process was then repeated a few more times, with the initial cups staying adhered. The sensation was mildly annoying, like a large earring pulling your lobe slightly past its comfort zone.

After about ninety seconds, Malik released each cup, creating a satisfying hissing sound.

"All done," he said.

I turned around to thank Malik for making my first cupping experience a pleasant one and was shocked to find Crystal behind me. She was handing Dr. Chuck some papers and I could swear she was looking at me.

"Your back is jacked, bro!" Than offered up.

I took a glance in the mirror behind me and counted nine red circles across my back and upper arm. Crystal must have been checking out the damage.

"Just wait until tomorrow," Dr. Chuck said from across the floor. "Red will be purple in an hour."

"You're all set," Malik said.

I pulled my shirt back over my head, stretching the collar as far as it would go to avoid further contact with my hair.

By the time I made my way back to the front desk, Crystal was there, typing away.

I handed her my debit card before she could ask for the $30 co-pay. I added that I wanted to schedule the rest of my appointments, which made her look up for a moment, taken by surprise.

"Looks like your health insurance has authorized you for six more appointments. Should I stick with the current schedule of Mondays, Wednesdays, and Fridays?" she asked.

"Yes, please, that would be great."

A few clanks on the keyboard and she looked up at me again. This time we locked eyes.

"You know, we had a new patient try to take your time slot, but I saved it, just in case you decided to see this through," she said.

I can't explain it, but suddenly, I felt like my best parts were looking back at me.

"Thanks," I said, surprised by the revelation. "I'm not usually great at sticking with things these days."

She slid my debit card back across the counter. "Sometimes we need someone to hold the space until we're ready to claim it."

"Sounds like something Mel Robbins would say," I said.

A smile broke across her face—not the practiced receptionist smile, but something genuine that reached her eyes.

The door squeaked as another patient entered, one I had never seen before, and Crystal's professional demeanor returned.

"All set for the next few weeks," she said, handing me a reminder card for the first time since therapy began.

Walking to my car, I caught myself swinging both arms naturally as I reached for my keys with my left hand—an act that would have sent sharp pain through my shoulder just weeks ago. I couldn't tell if the strange lightness in my legs was from the cupping therapy or from knowing Crystal had thought to hold my appointments. Either way, for the first time in a long time, I felt some of my bruises beginning to heal.

That night, I found myself on the treadmill at home for the first time in a year, maybe longer. I ran and ran and ran until the sweat hit the black deck below. My mind was empty, my legs were free. Afterward, I guzzled down a gallon of Poland Spring and did my at-home PT routine. I flicked the light on in my home office, grabbed a spiral-bound notebook, and flipped to a fresh blank page.

My plan was to make a list of things I needed to do over the coming week, but for whatever reason, instead of writing down that I needed milk for Ben's visit next weekend, and that I needed to pay the landscaper the overdue invoice, I made a list of people. People that I needed to call. People that I wanted to see. People that I knew I would never have to deal with again. It wasn't a long list, but one name stood out with stars around it: Crystal.

The sun was setting on a decent day, and for the first time in a very long time, I felt excited about tomorrow. Not to mention I had zero shoulder pain. I picked up my newly delivered copy of *Let Them* and read until I drifted into a deep and steady sleep.

A SPECK OF ADVENTURE

My neighbor Mark Coyle died. It struck me as odd because he was a sturdy man. Couldn't have been more than sixty-five. Not fit per se, but he was always clear-eyed and lucid, up-to-date on the latest in politics and technology.

Our conversations were infrequent: brief and always hovering at the surface. A morning wave. Some weather talk. Maybe a complaint or two about the asshole in the White House. But I didn't know Mark and Mark didn't know me, and it was clear that we both liked it that way. Anytime one of us lingered too long in small talk, the other would find a polite reason to slip away.

So when my phone rang last week and the caller ID revealed McConkey and Sons, which I assumed was spam, I let the call go to voicemail. Two minutes later, I read the transcript of the message.

"Hi, this call is for Anthony Anzalone. My name is Laurel McConkey and I am handling the estate of Mark Coyle.

There's a matter that we need to discuss. Please call me back at the number I called you from at your earliest convenience. Thank you."

My first move was to Google Mark's name to see if his death was public record yet. That would indicate this could be a scam. The search turned up nothing. But a search of "McConkey and Sons" did turn up a legitimate-looking website with a photo of three blue-eyed lads who looked like they would be McConkeys.

Though the tagline had a lot to be desired: Estate Planning and Elder Law: From bed sores to falls, we got you.

The phone number on the website matched the number that had called, so I phoned back. A receptionist named Rosa, who I pictured sitting behind a huge desk emblazoned with the name "McConkey" in neon lights, answered and patched me through to Laurel McConkey, who did not sound like one of the sons.

"Are you Anthony Anzalone?" Laurel asked.

"Yes."

"I called about the estate of Mark Coyle."

"Mark Coyle? That's...unexpected."

"You're listed as a beneficiary."

"This must be some kind of mix-up," I said.

"Were you not friends with Mr. Coyle?" she asked.

"Not really. I mean there was one time he rode out East and I fed his three cats some chicken and lamb-flavored kibble and cleaned out the litter box, but that was about the extent of it."

"Hmm," she said. Letting the silence sit just long enough to make me feel guilty for what was next.

"Well, depth of your relationship with Mr. Coyle aside, the deceased has determined that you will inherit..."

Her voice trailed off. It wasn't to build suspense, she genuinely sounded confused. "Interesting," she resumed. "Your neighbor has left you Pride and Joy, his two beloved motorcycles. We'll just need you to stop by the office to verify your identity and handle the paperwork to transfer ownership.

I was floored.

I couldn't believe that Mark left me anything, let alone something that I knew he loved so much.

He would spend hours polishing the chrome handlebars and exhaust pipes. Jockeying the hogs (is that what bikers call their bikes?) in and out of his garage depending on the weather. And disappearing for days at a time as he rode through upstate New York, on winding roads with his biker buddies.

Laurel McConkey roped me back in.

"Will sometime this week work to come in for the paperwork?" she asked.

We agreed on Tuesday and disconnected.

I've never ridden a motorcycle before. In fact, I quite hate them. The loud sounds. The dangerous speeds. Heck, come to think of it, I've never even sat on one. And frankly, anytime I heard Pride and Joy revving up, I would tell Becca, my wife, "Here comes Mr. Loud and Obnoxious."

That night, I tossed and turned. It wasn't dreams of my legs wrapped around a hunk of steel, hair blowing in the wind on the open road that kept me awake.

It was the why. Why did Mark choose me?

I replayed all of our conversations in my head.

The time he told me that the landlord keeps his rent down and lets him use the garage because he takes such great care of the place. I knew it was true, because whether he was mowing the green lawn, shoveling the white snow, or removing brown leaves from the gutters, Mark was always out doing something to keep the house in good standing.

"You take more pride in the house than a lot of folks around here," I told him.

"The banks own the houses anyhow. It's all about having respect for the space you inhabit," he said.

There was another conversation we had about a rumored break-in on the next street.

"Let them try that shit with me," he said firmly.

Never one for awkward silence, I reached for a platitude. "Some boundaries aren't meant to be crossed."

I didn't ask if Mark had a gun. Or if he was proficient in jiujitsu. I did what I always did and that was to serve up a neutral response and look to keep moving on with my day.

There was a morning in late October when Mark asked if I wanted any bulbs for my bare garden beds. He was dividing his tulips, had more than enough to share.

"I kill everything I plant," I said, which wasn't exactly true. I'd just never really tried. "Best I stick to my dirt patches."

He shrugged and went back to working the soil. The following spring, his yard erupted in yellow and white and pink, while mine stayed brown.

I had never asked a single question about the motorcycles. Or taken a tulip or a tomato or swig of beer. I used to tell myself that Mark and I liked our distance—that it was easier, cleaner, neighborly without being neighborly. But now, I wasn't so sure. Maybe I never showed real interest because I was too distracted, or too polite, or just assumed there'd always be time later. And now there wasn't. And that gnawed at me more than I expected it to.

I visualized myself riding Pride, then swapping to ride Joy. Watching the houses swirl by as I take the side roads to the beach as I get my sea legs. By the time I reach Ocean Avenue, I'm feeling more confident. I squeeze the throttle tighter, and the sand and waves to my right become parallel lines of beige and blue.

I finally slept but woke up tired.

The next morning, Becca laughed when I asked her how to dress for the lawyer visit.

"Do you still have those black leather chaps?" she chided.

"C'mon, Bec," I said. "Cut me some slack, this whole thing is just weird."

"Fine. Can I at least give you a cool biker name? Maybe Slider? Or Drifter? Oh. Got it. Terrible Tony! Double T for short."

The only thing Becca might love more than me is watching me in uncomfortable situations. I mean, nothing that would be harmful to me or the family. But watching me as confused as a Dallasite at a salad bar? Sign her up. And me with two motorcycles? Laughs for days. Maybe even weeks.

I combed my hair back and slipped on generic blue jeans, a black polo, and my gray New Balance dad shoes. Red socks, for just a touch of rebel.

The McConkey office was a ten-minute drive down Utopia Turnpike, in the next town over. As me and the Kia endured what felt like the seventeenth traffic light, I wondered how this drive would feel on a motorcycle. Would I use the space between the left and right lane to get places faster? Maybe ignore the "30 mph" traffic signs? Or would I just list the bikes on eBay and put the money in the bank for a rainy day?

I pulled into the office lot, finding it empty except for two cars: an immaculate gray Infinity SUV and an old green Honda Civic coupe that had to have been twenty years old. I parked between both and stepped inside.

The office directory in the vestibule only listed a single office: McConkey—suite 120. The other side of the glass doors led to a small lobby that revealed a large green plant and wooden double doors with gold lettering.

Not knowing what to expect on the other side, I took a deep breath and grabbed the door handle.

There was no "McConkey" written on the reception desk, just a woman about my age, who jumped when I entered.

"Sorry," I said. "I didn't mean to startle you."

She stared at me blankly for a moment, her pale blue eyes locked on mine. And then she laughed so hard she almost cried.

"You're the one with the appointment," she exclaimed. "Assuming you are Anthony Anzalone?"

"Live and in the flesh, ready to claim my crotch rockets."

I don't know what made me say something so stupid.

But this time, the lady laughed so hard she had to sit. As she pressed a Kleenex into her eyes, I noticed how perfect her teeth were. Not in a fake white veneer kind of way, just good old-fashioned nice teeth. And pretty eyes, the kind that surrounding crow's-feet somehow amplify.

She finally mustered the strength to stand and came around the desk to shake my hand.

"Laurel McConkey," she said. "Nice to meet you."

"Likewise," I said.

She motioned me through a tiny hallway to sit at a small wooden table that was loaded with manila envelopes.

"Now," Laurel said, pulling a thick folder from the stack. "I know this might seem overwhelming, but we'll take it step by step."

"Much appreciated," I said.

"Now, you had said on the phone that you barely knew Mark?"

"Yeah. We're just—

I caught myself tensing.

"We were just neighbors. No real relationship," I said.

"You are much younger than I expected," she said. "I mean, don't take this the wrong way, but you sounded pretty old and grumpy on the phone."

Her candor threw me for a loop.

"I dunno. Just nervous, I guess. I've never been left anything from a dead person before."

"Consider yourself lucky. Because you are not that young to not have known a few folks who have passed."

"Did you see that old green Civic out there?" she asked. "First thing I ever inherited. My uncle's. Everyone told me to sell it and buy something more professional, but..." She shrugged. "Sometimes the best gifts come with a little character."

She began walking me through the transfer paperwork, and I found myself oddly at ease. Maybe it was her ability to translate the dense paragraphs into human terms.

At one point, I leaned in and asked the question that had been burning in my mind.

"Any idea why Mark left these to me?"

"I'll be honest," she said. "I never met the man. He did everything virtually except for the notarization."

"I just find it so strange," I said.

"Can I be direct with you, Mr. Anzalone?" Laurel asked.

"Please," I replied.

She looked out the window and shifted her reading glasses on top of her head.

"You know, most people who sit in that chair are dealing with heavy things—loss, grief, tough decisions. They come here looking for closure. It's the end stages. But you? You're in a rare position, Mr. Anzalone. No debts to settle, no obligations to fulfill. Just possibility. Yet, I can see you searching these papers like they hold some secret message from Mark."

She stood from her desk and walked in my direction, smiled, and put a hand on my shoulder.

"Sometimes a gift is just a gift. And the only answer worth finding is what you're going to do with it."

And with that, she reached into her pocket and placed two sets of keys on the table.

I picked them up, surprised at how dainty the entry point to something so gruff could feel.

These weren't just keys to motorcycles. They were keys to something else entirely.

"Thank you," I said. "Looks like I have some figuring out to do."

"Yeah," Laurel said. "For starters, where are you taking your first ride?"

WHO IS TRAINING WHOM? AN INTERVIEW WITH AIDEN SULLIVAN

Setting: A twenty-eight-year-old working from his apartment, tagging images, transcribing audio, and classifying text for a large tech company's AI training program. His job is to teach machines how to see and understand the world. We met at the modern coffee shop located at the ground level of his apartment building.

Intro: Millions of AI models depend on human input. Every day, AIDEN sifts through thousands of images, audio clips, and text snippets—teaching machines to recognize our world. After two years in tech support and HR, he's embraced this digital assembly line. What keeps him clicking?

Q: Have you always worked from home?

A: Not always. But for this job, yes. The work is so repetitive that being around other people all day would be a distraction and likely lead to significant errors.

Q: Since you work in a relatively new field, for the casual reader, can you explain your work with artificial intelligence in simple terms?

A: Sure. At the core, it's simple. I am responsible for logging what I see, what I hear, and what I feel. Throughout the day, different media is put in front of me. I go into Swayze—that's the name of the platform that captures the front-end data to feed to Bodhi, which is the large language model that gobbles up all the info. So, like, today, I had to look through hundreds of images from a wedding in Delhi, and attach metadata to each: things like colors, emotions, names of people if identifiable, and so on. That information will ultimately determine which specific prompts will pull forward the image, or elements of it, for use in an answer to a query that a user has.

Q: Do you ever feel like you're invading anyone's privacy?

A: Anything that we model trainers get access to has been approved by the submitter. There are agreements and releases and everything, so it's not like we're seeing something that hasn't been approved. But I will say when I first started last year, I felt like a voyeur. Like, the wedding photos from this morning would have made me feel happy. Or curious. I'd wonder: Where did the bride grow up? Is the groom hiding some kind of dark secret? Heck, where do these people find the money to have these elaborate affairs? There were all of these unanswered questions. But then you realize the answers are irrelevant, at least to the task at hand. In fact, the answer could be dangerous, shading your answers toward bias, which is the one gray blob that ruins the entire AI experience.

Q: So, how do you handle that emotional detachment? Does it ever feel draining?

A: (Pauses.) I think it's the opposite. When you realize you have a job that forces you to check emotionality at the door, it becomes...freeing. It's like, now I'm not wasting *feelings* on the job, so I have that much more to give after work. More energy when I rock climb or hang out with the guys. Does that make sense?

Q: Yes. It's like keeping the supercharge in the chamber and only firing it after work.

A: Exactly. I don't think I ever realized how important it was to compartmentalize until this job. Doing what I do now might not be exciting or fun, but it also doesn't come along with the complexities that human relationships bring to the table. There's no resetting boundaries after having one too many at happy hour, or having to write up one of your friends at work for missing deadlines. I was in HR before this. But after a couple of years, I realized it was like working for a police state.

Q: What do you mean?

A: Like, the promise of human resources is that they are all about the people. But even the name itself frames workers as a means to an end, like two-legged cattle. You learn quickly on the inside that the only people HR are really there to serve are the ones who own the company. It's a field that just looks to check boxes and control people, working hand in hand with legal. Those days were draining. Wanting to vomit when helping an employee out with their lava lamp and picture frames filled with little kids, or needing to write someone up just because their boss won't accept generalized anxiety disorder as a real thing. It's an ugly space dotted with a few carnations here and there. My sleep suffered. My home life ached. It just wasn't for me. And actually, saying it aloud, just reinforces I'm in a much better place.

Q: So you enjoy the work. What's a piece of media you have processed that has stayed with you, for better or worse?

A: Oooof. For a short stretch, we were training the model based on transcripts between prisoners and visitors. I understand why all of the conversations are recorded. It's yet another right you lose when you are convicted of a crime. But the longing and desperation the inmates put on display, even knowing they may have an audience, was just brutal. There was one conversation, without getting too deep into the details, where a prisoner was begging his mother to find a way to smuggle in poison. He just couldn't adjust to prison life, and the conversation devolved into four or five people hysterically crying on the phone at the same time. It was brutal. Just brutal. I never searched to see if the prisoner was alive or dead because I was scared to find out he was still suffering.

Q: That is powerful. Thank you for sharing such a raw story. So, let me wrap up with one more question. Do you see yourself doing this in ten years?

A: I would do this ten years from now, but at that point we are way past the moment of singularity. Forget training the large language model; the model will be training us. Ten years from now I picture myself focused on manual labor. If there's still a world where we need bricklayers, I'll be there with mortar on my hands and the sun on my back, stacking one brick on top of the other.

A PLASTIC PAUSE

Connor stared at the humongous fish tank that severed the restaurant in two.

A small treasure chest overfilled with bubbles, each rising to the surface to die. And as he watched a small school of neon tetras glide aimlessly, he realized that he would give anything to swim through the synthetic tendrils of plastic seaweed.

"Do you even hear what I'm saying?" Michael asked. "'Cause I'll tell you what, Con, you're running out of time, and the answer is sure as hell not in that tank."

Connor wished the answer was in the tank, buried under fish shit and gravel.

His older brother, Mike, meant well, but the conversation was going to result in nothing more than rows of neatly arranged sugar packets, tiny anthills of salt, and a better understanding of contained aquatics.

The decision was simply too big for one person to make. But it was his call, and his alone.

Throughout their childhood, Mike had always kept a watchful eye on Con while their parents encased themselves in selfish bubbles that floated in opposite directions. By no means was he a surrogate father, but Mike was there without fail when it counted the most.

Like the time John Tsopalis shoved Connor's floral baseball hat into the big blue mailbox, only to show up the next day with a gash on his face.

Or when Nellie Smythe broke Connor's heart for the third time and Mike took him to the batting cage where they feasted on pizza squares and an ice cold pitcher of Killian's Red.

He hated having to do this. The gratitude and guilt mixed together like chicken and broccoli. The gravy-soaked white rice heavy on the fork, mirroring Connor's apprehension.

The waiter, with a face that looked like he had been a waiter for sixty years, sauntered over to the rickety plastic table that was desperately masquerading as wood and announced that the pair looked like they could use some dessert.

Connor needed a lot more than that.

"Why not try our new dessert bento box with sweet coconut sushi rice, candied wasabi, ginger—"

"No thanks," Mike snapped, instantly realizing that the waiter was taking this all way too personally.

"I think we're cool, right, Con?"

"Yeah. We'll just take the check, please."

ALL STORIES BY DREW G. ROSEN

And like a tired magician, the waiter pulled the bill from behind his back, some chocolate-covered fortune cookies from his front pocket, and placed them in the center of the table, muttering something about how he hoped the gentlemen would dine with them again.

Connor paid, it was the least he could do.

Mike struggled against the wind to open the trembling restaurant door, and when he finally did, it was worth the fight. The autumn air had prematurely evolved to winter chill status as if it had missed the message that Halloween had yet to pass. After sitting in the stifling restaurant for more than two hours waiting for a response from his younger brother, Mike's clenched jaw, deep crow's-feet, and white knuckles told the story. He was pissed.

"Wow, by the time you finally give me an answer, it'll be the fucking dead of winter," he said, as he kicked some crushed gray rocks into the air.

Michael and Connor both knew this was by far the toughest decision they would ever have to make, and each blamed the pressure that consumed him on the other. Their individual frustrations boiled over and foamed down to the pilot light, where every ounce of anger was corralled into a reservoir that begged for release. Connor, with his hand on the valve, knew this was no different than open-heart surgery: likely a success, but glaring with the indistinct risks and uncertainties that each patient brought to the surgical table.

"Feel that?" asked Mike. "Even the wind has had enough of your indecision."

They climbed into the little Honda with the rusted bumper and the wind rocked it back and forth like a clueless first-time dad trying to get his son down for the night. Connor was not only contending with his older brother for an answer, but the elements were soliciting for closure as well.

Even though they weren't speaking, the rattle and hum of the car, coupled with the fiercest winds either of them could recall, filled the space with a thick, solid, and persistent sound. The faint smell of fried noodles and old tea stuck to them like unwelcome passengers.

A large plastic garbage can clumsily tumbled into the middle of the road and stopped the brothers dead in their tracks. The blue Rubbermaid with the "Please Recycle" sticker stared the Honda down.

The trees continued to shake and wobble as yellowish orange leaves accumulated on the cold, hard pavement. Streetlights swayed like hammocks as red and green trails of light offered the opportunity to neither stop nor go. The world was twirling as they sat suspended, waiting for the garbage can to blow out of their way. Traffic flowed all around the two young men who had somehow managed to get themselves in a one-car jam.

The standoff between plastic and man froze time just long enough.

Connor knew what he had to do. Life for him and Mike would never be the same.

VANILLA PHONES: AN INTERVIEW WITH GABE MORENO

Setting: A brightly lit cell phone store. LED lights everywhere. Phones on display. Minimalist and modern store, bordering on clinical. Customer traffic appears slow, until everyone comes in at once.

Intro: Smartphones are ubiquitous. And despite online commerce accounting for a majority of retail sales across the United States, 41 percent of Americans prefer to buy their pocket computers from a brick and mortar store. GABE has worked for two other wireless carriers, Tech Talk being his third stop this year. What keeps him coming back to the retail cell phone space?

Q: What do you like about your job?
A: Can I say the girls? For real, It's dope. They come in all day long, and once you help them, you never need to

ask for their number. (Laughs, big wide smile.) I'm kidding, of course, I would never text them without permission first. But low-key, Gary, the manager kind of sucks. But he's in Cancun this week on a company retreat, so *¡es hora de fiesta!*

Q: But what really keeps you here? Third carrier this year—that's a lot of movement.

A: (Shifts, gets a little defensive.) Look, I'm good at this, all right? Like, really good. I can read people in thirty seconds—know if they want the newest thing or just something that works. The other places, management was trash, but here... I've got my numbers down. I know what I'm doing.

And honestly? It's not like I'm flipping burgers. This requires skill. You gotta understand tech, read people, handle complaints. Gary acts like anyone can do this, but I see the new hires wash out every month.

Q: What don't you like about the job?

A: I mean, it's cell phones. They're all the same, but I have to make the new ones sound like they are the best. Gorilla Glass this and AI that. It's thinner, it's lighter, it folds, it bends, it bounces. You know, it's like selling someone water. The only difference is the bottle and the label. And anyone under fifty has done their research and they come in here like they gotta be Matlock and stump you, ya know? Like, dude, I make fourteen dollars an hour and get a thirty-five-minute lunch break, do you think I give a shit about how the phone feels in your hand when you're texting your side piece? So I guess it's the fake enthusiasm. You burn out if you don't pace it. You say the same stuff so often that you forget you're lying.

(Pause.) Actually, that's the weird part. Sometimes I catch myself believing my own pitch. Like, I'll be explaining some camera feature and think, "Damn, that is pretty cool." Then I remember I said the exact same thing about last year's model. I hate that I'm good at convincing people they need shit they don't need. But I also... I dunno, I like being good at something.

Oh, and you know what? Inventory. That's the worst. Last month we had to come in early, stay late, and watch as this guy from HQ scans every box we got in the back. Every SIM card. Every case and screen protector. And then we get an action plan the next day. Stack the phones differently. Keep the doors locked. Fucking reminders hung everywhere. Sorry, I probably shouldn't curse. But it was like they moved things just for the sake of moving things. I hate that.

Q: Ever have a customer who surprised you?

A: Yeah. There was this older lady—came in with an iPhone 13, couldn't figure out how to use the home screen. I'm standing there, thinking, Why are we stuck here? Turns out she'd taken like, a million screenshots of her home screen by accident. Just pages and pages of the same thing.

While I was helping her delete them, she told me her daughter was deployed. All she wanted was to send a text and make sure she was okay.

So I wrote down the steps on a sticky note—real basic. Home, messages, type, send. She texted her daughter right then. Got a reply from Germany in under two minutes. Then boom—FaceTime. Her daughter called to thank me for helping her mom.

(Laughs, scratches back of his head.) I was like, okay, that's kinda cool.

Q: Moments like that—do they change how you feel about the work?

A: (Long pause.) Yeah, but then I remember that lady probably could've figured it out herself if she watched a You-Tube video. Or asked her neighbor. She didn't need to spend two hours here and buy a forty-dollar case she'll never use.

But... I mean, she was happy. Her daughter was happy. Maybe that counts for something? (Shrugs uncomfortably.) I don't know. Most days it's just moving product. But sometimes...sometimes I actually help people. Even if they're overpaying for the privilege.

Q: You mentioned this is your third carrier this year. What happened at the other places?

A: First place, the manager was a control freak. Second place, they promised a commission structure they never delivered on. But honestly? (Looks around.) Maybe I get restless. Like, once I figure out the system, once

I know I can hit my numbers, it gets...boring? Or maybe I start seeing all the bullshit too clearly.

Here, I've lasted longer than anywhere else. Fourteen months. That's a record for me. Sometimes I wonder if I'm just scared to try something else. What if I'm not good at anything but selling phones?

Q: If you could do anything else tomorrow—no pressure, no bills—what would it be?

A: Man...I'd probably sleep in. Get tacos. Play old-school Mario Kart. Just dumb fun, no schedule. Then I'd swing by here just to watch Gary melt down on the sales floor without me. That alone might be worth it. (Laughs.)

But if I'm being real? I don't know. I used to mess around with music—beats, samples, that kind of thing. Had the software, a whole setup in my room. But there's always someone better, or faster, or who already has, like, a connection. This job...I dunno...you show up, look busy, and it's pretty easy not to care. (Pause.) I mean...I care a little. Just not enough to make it harder.

Q: When you say you "care a little"—what does that mean?

A: (Fidgets with display phone.) I guess...I care about doing it right when I'm here. I care about my numbers. I care when customers actually leave happy instead of feeling ripped off. But caring too much about a job selling phones? That seems dangerous. Like, what happens when they decide to close this location, or when Gary decides he doesn't like me?

My mom always asks when I'm going back to school, when I'm gonna "apply myself." But she doesn't get it—I am applying myself. I'm just applying myself to something she doesn't think counts. And maybe...maybe she's right? But at least here I know I'm good at what I do. Even if what I do is sell people water in different bottles.

DROPKICKS AND DINKS

One Sunday morning in the middle of March, Danny De-Marco's agent, with strain in her voice, called to tell him that his active roster contract was unlikely to be renewed. Instead, he would be offered a "superannuated deal," which essentially was the company's way of taking care of their washed-up stars. *Thanks for the memories, Grandpa.*

Danny's brain knew it was a good deal: make a few appearances a year, continue to get a salary, full medical, and access to all company training facilities—a token of appreciation for a willingness to destroy your body. But his heart wanted to piledrive the offer right up the CEO's twenty-seven-year-old ass.

He ended the call saying he'd think about it, a thinly-veiled threat that he could still sign with the upstart league that was desperate to sign recognizable names.

"Nobody gets to do their finisher on retirement, it always gets the final move on you," Mike Bennett, the long-time 1980s Intercontinental champion once told Danny and the other rookies during the Legends lecture series. That was before Mike was quickly ushered offstage by Sal Ionetta, the president of wrestling operations for Global Fighting.

That was thirty-one years ago, and it was just about the only thing Danny remembered before he became Danny "Deadpan" DeMarco.

The name started as a joke. A bunch of guys backstage thought it would be funny if Danny entered the raucous Beacham Hall with sad music, no expression, and no personality. Always one to accept a challenge, Danny dove in headfirst. During the short walk from the lockers to the ragged ring, which was about two feet too short, Danny felt something empowering about holding back from the audience.

The tension between him and twelve hundred people was taut, as if he was holding back the answer to a riddle the crowd was desperate to know. His opponent, the Ninja Kid, got him in a headlock, and with his hair draped over both of them, whispered, "What the fuck, Danny?" He didn't answer, just went through the sequence of moves they had rehearsed.

The only change was that there was no acting. No letting the people see his pain when Ninja slapped him across the chest. No celebrating when he hit a diving headbutt off the top rope to put his opponent at the brink of defeat. The only sign of life came when Danny locked in his closing move, a sleeper hold, in the center of the ring. As his arm wrapped around Ninja's neck, he looked out to the crowd for the first time and unleashed a laugh.

ALL STORIES BY DREW G. ROSEN

The laugh.

The one that would follow him during career highs and lows. A maniacal cackle that sounded like an evil hyena supervillain who was left dying on the cutting room floor at DC Comics.

The sleeper hold locked in, Ninja tapped out, and the crowd roared with a shock of laughter. Danny slipped back into "Deadpan" mode and slowly strode back to the dressing room.

The guys backstage were dying—death by giggle. The crew was laughing. And when Sal got in Danny's face, demanding, "What the fuck was that?" Danny just went to his locker, stiff as a board, gathered his stuff in a large green duffel bag, and left the arena—not through the backstage area—but through the crowd.

A legend was born.

Later that night, Sal called with a three-year-contract offer, to which Danny deadpanned, "Sure."

Thirty-one years, seventeen countries, four concussions, and one very expensive divorce later, the Laugh Lock had become both a trademark (owned by Global Fighting) and a curse. People still asked for it. At airports, grocery stores, and once, at his mother's funeral. And now it was at the end of the line, being put out to pasture with full medical.

***

Danny never minded the grind. What he hated were the inevitable injuries, which led to inexorable rehab.

He could never get his mind in the right place.

Somewhere around the two hundredth repetition of some stretch band exercise, his thoughts would start circling the drain.

Why'd he marry Sue when he knew it would end ugly? He should've just been a plumber like his dad. Why the hell did he let his entire life get reduced to a gimmick—a joke?

His shoulder pain had hovered at a seven out of ten for the past two decades, but after taking a hard hit from Quandry—a new kid just called up from the developmental league—it jumped to a nine.

The company orthopedist, Dr. Nuss, a nebbishy thirty-year-old who clearly had never taken a bump in his life, called it "accelerated degenerative wear."

No shit, Danny thought. That's what decades of whams, bams, and slams will get you.

So, once again, it was off to physical therapy. But since the corporate rehab center was under renovation, he'd been rerouted to Big Guava PT—a strip-mall clinic sandwiched between a nail salon and a carpet store.

Mornings had gotten weird lately. They were quiet but not in a peaceful way. There was always a buzz in his ears, the opening salvo to a new day that would eventually feel like the same old day.

He'd wake up around seven, not because he had to, but because that's when his body hurt the most. There were no flights to catch, no matches to prepare for, no

ALL STORIES BY DREW G. ROSEN

call sheets or weigh-ins or late-night production meetings. Just a condo that smelled faintly of beef and broccoli and a constant metallic hum in his head.

The waiting room at Big Guava smelled like cinnamon gum and hand sanitizer. It was so white it was blue.

Danny stood at the check-in desk behind an older woman in tennis gear who looked like she'd just come from some Tampa tournament. The receptionist, a girl bundled up like she was prepping for a Vermont winter, couldn't have been more than twenty. She handed him a clipboard with a bright smile.

He took a seat in the far corner. As he filled out the forms and wrote his name nine times in multiple places for reasons no sane person could explain, the tennis lady leaned over.

"Aren't these forms nuts? Just bonkers."

Danny gave her a small grin and nodded.

"What are you in for?" she asked.

Great, he thought. Recognition. But as he studied her face, weathered from the Florida sun, he pegged her at around sixty-five. Probably too old to care about wrestling—unless she had grandkids looking for an autograph.

"Just some shoulder stuff," he offered.

"From sports?" she asked. "You look active."

"Yeah. Some angry wrestling injuries from the past have come to cash in."

"I get it," she said. "At eighty-two, I never realized how often the piper comes looking to get paid. I used to think the key to staying young was brainteasers and a clean diet, but I've learned the real secret to life. Want to hear it?"

Danny did want to hear it. If she really was eighty-two, and looked as fit as she did, she knew something. "Hit me."

"Pickleball," she said.

"Pickleball?"

"Yup. Life is that simple. Pickleball keeps the body limber, the mind sharp, and—most important—it gives you people. Camaraderie, competition, connection. You can't find that in a crossword puzzle."

She smiled, clearly rehearsed but still sincere.

"It's inclusive, too," she added. "One day you lose to a sixty-year-old with his gut spilling over his shorts, the next you beat a cocky twenty-year-old who thinks his tennis game will carry over. Pickleball is a sport that humbles everybody."

"I'm not sure I need more humbling these days," Danny said.

Pickleball Lady reached into her fanny pack and pulled out a small laminated business card.

"We play at the public courts up on Overbrook Ave.," she said, handing it to him. "Open play. Mondays, Wednesdays, Fridays. First session's free. We have paddles and balls. Just show up with sneakers and an open mind."

Danny took the card. Nodded. Slipped it into his back pocket to be polite.

"Claire, we're ready for you," the receptionist said.

"Name's Claire," she said as she passed by to see the doctor. "Hope to see you out there, Danny."

She gave a wink and shuffled off. He hadn't told her his name.

***

That night, back at the condo, Danny microwaved leftover pepper steak and brown rice and watched the steam fog up the microwave window. He didn't move until the oven beeped.

A soft whistle echoed from across the room.

"Hold on, Jobber," Danny muttered.

He walked to the corner cage where a yellow parakeet shuffled along its perch. Never could've had one of these on the road, he thought. Could barely remember toothpaste, let alone keep something alive.

Danny opened the lid and gently refreshed the water dish, then crumbled in a few seeds from a plastic container marked *Flock of Forage*.

"You got no idea how good you've got it," Danny said. "Rent's paid, no concussions, nobody asking you to fall backward off a twenty-foot ladder."

Jobber chirped once and fluffed her feathers like a shrug.

He emptied his jeans pockets onto the coffee table: keys, loose change, and a business card.

Claire Keats – Pickleball Coach – 813-PKL-PLAY

The card sat there like a dare.

Danny felt twenty years too young for pickleball. He also felt twenty years too old to lace up the boots and climb back into a wrestling ring.

Sinking into his recliner, he turned on the TV, immediately lowered the volume, and stared at the closed captions for a few minutes. He had seen this episode a hundred times, the one where the couch won't fit through the door so the neighbors gather to unstuff the cushions.

Thumbing through his phone between bites of two-day old meat, he read that the rag sheets were predicting a huge heel turn at next week's Freedom FreeFall III. The focus was on Chaz Lazer, the company's twenty-four-year-old golden boy, the latest superhero-looking fan favorite to have bleach blond hair and hold the World Heavyweight title.

Danny checked his text messages and emails, finding nothing new except for a few messages from his agent, Jane, which he ignored, and a code for 10 percent off at Protein Universe.

He stared at the ceiling for a few minutes, then tapped his phone to one of the few names still in his Favorites: Rich Britchard.

Rich picked up on the second ring.

"Deadpan! What's up, legend?"

"Just checking in. You good?"

"Me? Never better. I'm flying to Omaha next weekend. Indie show at the VFW. Three hundred bucks and hot catering. Still livin' the dream, baby."

Danny let out a tired snort through his nose. "How's the back?"

"Dude, it's shot. Can't sit, can't sneeze. But I can still take a bump from the top rope if my dance partner knows how to tango. Anyway, what about you? You gonna take the retirement package?"

"Still weighing options."

"Don't waste the chance, Danny. You'll miss the lights, the crowds, the brothers—we all do. But ignoring Father Time is a fool's mistake."

They talked for another minute. About nothing.

When Danny hung up, the condo was quiet again. He dozed off, imagining smashing a pickleball paddle in Chaz Lazer's face and leaving with the belt.

***

Danny sat in his pickup truck outside of the Overbrook Avenue pickleball courts and watched the mismatched lineup of players doing some of the most ineffective stretches he had ever seen. From his vantage point, the group appeared to be mostly retirees, with a few stray middle-aged folks and college kids mixed in.

He looked down at his worn-out sneakers and baggy shorts.

"This is so stupid," he said aloud to no one.

And that's when Claire tapped the handle of her paddle on the driver's side window.

"You gonna come play with us or what? You don't strike me as a guy who just likes to watch."

***

The group did not look like athletes, though they sure had the knee braces and headbands to play the part.

After a quick explanation of the rules, all of which made sense (except the scoring seemed unnecessarily complicated), Claire walked him over to the far court, where the two of them tapped the ball back and forth to each other.

"Congrats," she said. "You're pretty good at dinking."

The dink, Danny learned, was the foundation of the sport.

"It's not exciting or flashy," Claire said. "But it's a key ingredient to setting up a point."

"Kinda like technical mat work," Danny said. "Ain't no one paying to see you roll on the ground, but the stalling makes the eventual suplex that much more exciting."

Claire nodded at his comparison, maybe impressed, maybe just polite.

"All right, time to see how you handle an actual point," she said.

Then she turned and waved over a couple of players waiting nearby.

A guy in high white socks and a tie-dyed visor jogged over with a woman in a bright purple tank top and neon pink sneakers. Danny had more muscle in one arm than these two had combined. But they might be over with the crowd because they looked like pickleball players.

"Holy shit, you're Deadpan DeMarco," said Visor Guy.

"Guilty," Danny said.

"Do the thing!" the man demanded.

Claire and the other woman looked disgusted, as if Visor Guy had melted into a man-child right before their eyes. What they didn't realize is that professional wrestling is the gift that allows grown men and women to retreat to childhood.

Danny was embarrassed to be recognized but figured the sooner he did the laugh, the sooner he could get on with smashing the ball down this dude's throat.

"HAHAHAHAHAHA."

"Awesome!" the man said grinning ear to ear. "Pleased to meet you. I'm Ben."

The men shook hands and Claire came over to Danny's side of the court.

"Ginger, you're with Ben. And go easy—this is literally Danny's first point. He's still figuring out which end of the paddle is which."

Danny took his spot back at the baseline and was pretty sure he felt butterflies. He dismissed the thought. He'd been the main event in front of fifty-five thousand screaming fans. There's no way some backyard game of Ping-Pong on steroids is gonna make me flinch, he thought.

Ben served and the ball floated over the net, the soft *pop* of the paddle against the plastic echoing surprisingly loud in the morning stillness. Danny took three aggressive steps forward and cracked it as hard as he could down the middle.

"Out!" Ginger called cheerfully.

"Okay, not bad!" Ben shouted, clearly impressed with the velocity, not the aim. "But remember—you gotta let it bounce first. That's the two-bounce rule."

"Right," Danny said. "I was just...testing the court."

Claire smiled without looking at him. Sure you were, she thought.

They reset.

Ben served again, this time toward Danny's backhand. Danny lunged and flicked it back, only for Ben to trot forward and dink it just over the net.

Danny tapped it back.

"You can't do that!" Ben cried.

"No," Claire said, stepping toward Danny. "That's the kitchen. Remember, if you step inside that zone, you can't hit the ball on a fly."

Danny looked down at the faded line near the net. "So...no smashing?"

"Not unless you earn it," Claire said. "Takes patience. And touch."

"Terrific," Danny muttered. "My two greatest qualities."

Ben beamed. "Don't worry, big guy—we'll bring out your inner baller. Just give it some time."

Danny adjusted his grip and stepped back into position. He noticed a few people pointing and laughing from across the park.

"Not bad for a rookie," Claire said, as she took a swig from her large water bottle that said, *Pickle Juice Inside.*

Danny had lost 11-1, 11-3, 11-2. And that was *with* Claire as his partner carrying the weight. His shirt clung to him with sweat. His paddle felt heavier now, like it was made of concrete.

"Any tips?" Danny asked the group.

Slow down and aim for the feet.

Stay low. And when you get home, Google "third shot drop."

Serve deep and get your ass right to the net.

He couldn't remember the last time people gave him advice without trying to sell something, steal something, or use it against him later.

The feeling was somewhat familiar, though. Almost like back in the day, riding buses overnight with the guys, trading ace bandages and ibuprofen like industry secrets.

These pickleball players were a helpful bunch. And once Danny realized they didn't care who he was or where he came from, he was able to relax in a way he hadn't in a long time.

***

Two days later, Danny showed up in new Adidas tennis sneakers, fitted shorts, and a shiny new paddle, which the woman at the store told him would give his game more control. He drew the line at a white dad hat.

"Well, well, well, at least now you look the part," Ben chided.

"HAHAHAHAHAHA," Danny "Deadpan" responded.

"What the heck was that?" asked another player.

"Nicole, meet Danny DeMarco, former wrestling champion and current pickleball rookie," said Ben.

Danny held out his paddle and Nicole tapped it.

"Nice to meet you," she said.

"Likewise."

Claire appeared behind the group of a dozen or so people. Each eagerly waiting for her to unlock the courts. She'd convinced the town mayor to let them access the courts early. "Let's just say he owes me a favor," she said with a wink.

As Claire handed out the court assignments, she told Danny, "Sorry, you're stuck with me again."

Their opponents were Sandy and Steve, a married couple who recently retired to Tampa from Long Island. He was struggling with the heat and she was missing good pizza. Danny tipped her off to Mama Ciro's in East Lake. "It's not New York pizza, but it's the closest you're going to get on this side of the bay," he promised.

Halfway through the match, with the team of Danny and Claire down 6-0, Sandy returned the kindness.

"Stop thinking so much," she said. "Just hit the ball back consistently and let us make the mistake. This is a game of patience."

In the ring, hesitation got you booed. You weren't there to wait—you were there to hit first, fly high, and give the crowd something to remember. It seemed like this pickleball thing might be the polar opposite.

After a couple of decent rallies, Danny lost the game 11-2, but a look from Claire boosted his confidence. While the box score didn't tell the story, he felt like he was getting the hang of the game.

"Thatta boy," Claire said as she leaned into him. "Use your conditioning and consistency to tire them out. They are not used to the heat of the sunshine state."

She bent down to scoop up a ball and added, more softly, "I moved down here with my wife, Gwen, just before she got sick. After she passed, I didn't know what to do with myself. The house felt like a museum—frozen in time."

She stood up again, looking toward the courts. "Then I found this game. And it helped. But the people, they are the ones who saved me."

Danny didn't say anything, just gave a small nod as they walked back to the baseline.

Lo and behold, the next game was a firefight, not in the physical sense, but it was a battle of will. With each passing point, Danny felt his heart not pounding in his chest, but leaning into the game ever so gently.

A twenty-one-shot rally ended with him dropping the softest dink into the kitchen, a shot that might as well have been a mile away from his opponents. It was so satisfying that Danny let out a "YES!"

"It's okay to enjoy yourself," encouraged Claire.

Danny was starting to realize that pickleball had its own rhythm: the hollow percussion of paddle meeting ball, the shuffling dance of players advancing and retreating, all moving within the tight confines of a court too small for ego but just right for connection.

He checked his phone between games. Another message from his agent. *Need your answer. It's gotta be "yes."* The thought made his stomach turn. Was it really retirement if your name got announced, then you waved from the ramp while someone else soaked up the crowd?

With pickleball, there was no pop. No pyro. No ring announcer screaming his name.

And yet...for the first time in a long time he was feeling things. Good things.

***

Over the next few weeks, Danny kept showing up every Monday, Wednesday, and Friday. He was always hydrated, and becoming increasingly hard to beat.

"We created a monster," Ben joked.

But he wasn't joking.

If the pickleball crew knew Deadpan from back in the day, they would recognize that look in his eyes. The one that says, *I'm all in, prepare to lose.*

Even Rich heard it in his voice the other night during a late-night chat.

"You sound like you're in a good place, brother," he said.

"Ever play pickleball?" Danny asked.

"Shit. Even I'm too young for that," Rich said.

Hard and soft, fast and slow. Spin to the left, spin to the right. Hit deep, go shallow. Danny found that keeping his game inconsistent was a weapon.

The points started to add up.

So did the victories.

And the laughs.

"Holy shit, Ben. Your face on that last ATP was priceless," Danny laughed. "Like a kid who just got his pants pulled down in front of the class."

Ben turned to his partner, William, a retired lawyer with a thick Boston accent who covered his face with his paddle to hide that he was beet red with laughter.

"Keep playing like that, Daniel, and Ben might be forced back to full-time golf," William said.

Danny grinned.

"Ya know," Ben said. "I think I liked you better as Deadpan—when you sucked at pickleball."

***

One of the things Danny missed the most about the spotlight of the squared circle was the focus it required. No time to think about bad business deals, late payments, or phone calls to return. No time to examine how every hotel stay drifts you further from family. And no time to worry about the body parts that are waving the white towel.

Pickleball was similar in that it required attention to the present moment, but at a much smaller price.

***

A couple of weeks later, Claire introduced her latest recruit to the group, Joey Mancini, a former D3 tennis player who wanted to see what his grandparents' hobby was all about.

"You ever play before?" asked William.

"Nah, but I watched some YouTube videos and I get it," Joey said.

The kid followed Claire to court three, where she always brought the new blood first.

Even from across the courts, Danny could tell—this kid had wheels. Fluid, fast, and way too comfortable for a first-timer.

"Whoa!" said Ben, looking at Danny. "Looks like you're going to have some competition."

Danny waved him off as he reached for his phone, which was buzzing inside his pickleball bag.

Jane. His agent. Missed call.

He had a new email notification, too.

Re: *Legends Contract—Final Deadline Approaching*

Whatever, he thought, and silenced the phone before putting it away.

"Great shot!" Claire yelled, as Joey held his arms up in victory formation.

Two games later, Danny found himself partnered with Ben across the net from William and Joey Mancini.

Claire had called out the matchup casually—"Let's mix things up!"—but it felt like something else. Like a test.

ALL STORIES BY DREW G. ROSEN

Joey bounced on his toes. Wore mirrored sunglasses. Had hair that flopped outside the parameters of his yellow headband.

"Hope I can keep up," Joey said, smirking.

"I'll try not to break a hip," Danny replied.

The first few points were fast. Too fast. Danny didn't have time to think, only react. And that was a problem.

Joey moved with a kind of slippery confidence, and somehow made every shot look like an accident and a miracle at the same time.

Danny tried to power through. He smacked a serve deep. Then rushed the net too early and clipped the ball into it.

"Gotta let it bounce," Joey said, grinning.

Danny didn't answer. His shoulder ached. His legs weren't listening.

A few more rallies, and it was 7-1, Team Joey.

On the next point, Danny lunged for a crosscourt shot, slipped on the court, and landed hard on his side. The thud echoed.

"WHOA. You okay?" Claire called out.

Danny waved her off and stayed down an extra second, eyes closed, waiting for the embarrassment to peak.

Joey walked over, extended a hand. "Sorry, man. You good?"

Danny looked up at him and took his hand. Young, lean, helpful. *The future.*

"Yeah," he said. "Just checking for loose screws."

The game didn't resume. Claire forced a water break.

"The thing with pickleball," she coached Danny, "is that there's always going to be someone better. The trick is to just stick to your game, no matter what your opponent dishes out. Surely you can relate to that?"

But Danny wasn't listening. His mind was on his sore lower back. And an autograph signing he had committed to a year ago.

***

That night, Danny couldn't stop thinking about Joey Mancini's pickleball game. It wasn't the power—it was the ease. Like he'd been playing the game forever.

It reminded him of the Brawl in Brooklyn a few years back—a pay-per-view main event where the company put him up against REX, the CEO's latest golden boy. Shredded physique. Millions of followers on social. Son of Santa Collins, the three-time champ from back in the territory days.

The locker room rolled their eyes. Another silver-spoon rookie skipping the line, being fast-tracked to the top. Danny figured he'd do what the veterans always did—slow it down, call it in the ring, make the kid look good but remind the crowd who the real pro was.

But REX didn't need help.

From the opening bell, he moved like lightning. Crisp. Confident. Polished in a way Danny hadn't expected. Not cocky—just *ready*. And for the first time in his career, Danny felt like he was a step behind. Not because the kid was unsafe or out of control. But because he was just...better.

ALL STORIES BY DREW G. ROSEN

After the match, Danny sat on a folding chair in the corner of the locker room and watched REX do a post-match interview on the monitor. The kid spoke clearly. Hit all the beats. Looked right into the camera like he was born there.

That was the first time Danny thought, Maybe this is almost over.

"There's no one to blame when time beats you clean," Rich had once said during one of their late-night chats.

Danny's heart knew there would always be a REX, always be a Joey Mancini, but that didn't make it any less of a dry horse pill to swallow.

***

Danny didn't show up to pickleball on Monday.

Or Wednesday.

He told himself it was his back. The humidity. He needed to trim Jobber's nails. But really, it was the way Joey moved. How could he compete with youth? It was a movie Danny had already seen: new guys with no scars, no limps, just endless stamina and agility.

He wasn't mad at Joey.

He just didn't want to face reality.

***

On Friday, after much debate and self-talk, Danny returned to the courts. His plan was to bring it back to basics. Focus on the ball and tune out everything else: classic Deadpan.

Much to his surprise (and delight), Joey was nowhere in sight.

He greeted Ben, William, and the others and they got to playing.

Maybe it was how good his back felt or the lack of humidity, but Danny played his best pickleball yet.

"Looks like someone is locked in after a few days off," Ben said.

Claire appeared and tossed Danny a spare paddle.

"You've been running the table lately. Time to give back."

Danny caught it, confused. "You want me to coach now?"

"Just think about someone who could use it," she said. "Someone who needs a place to move around. Bring them with you next time."

**

Jobber chirped happily, eating a small suet cake as Danny stared at his contacts. Scrolled past Sue. Past his accountant. Past Rich.

Then he saw it.

Terry Tides, cell

He hadn't spoken to Terry in years. The last time they crossed paths was at a fan expo in Milwaukee. Terry was in baggy maroon sweatpants and a sleeveless white Trixter shirt, limping. His autograph line was short and his patience even shorter.

"Those bastards took and took and took, and now look. I'm an old man with a broken body and smashed spirit."

Danny called. The phone hadn't even completed a ring when Terry picked up.

***

On Monday morning, Terry Tides arrived at the pickleball courts in blue denim shorts, an American flag bandana, and worn-out work boots.

"Jesus Christ," Ben muttered, nudging William. "It's the Barnyard Brawler."

Danny, stretching near the fence, didn't say anything.

Terry walked over, dragging his feet slightly. "So, is this the place where you find inner peace and shit?"

"Something like that," Danny said.

Claire walked over from the far court. "And who do we have here, Danny?"

"Everybody, meet Terry. He doesn't know how to play pickleball, but he once lost a steel-cage match to a guy dressed as a pickle."

"Gary Gherkin," Terry added. "He had that damn Dill-Dozer finisher. Hurt like a bitch, every time."

Claire extended her hand. "It's great to have you, Terry. Want to come with me so I can show you the basics?"

"Danny tells me I have no choice," he said, shooting his old wrestling friend a dirty look.

"I promise, no headlocks," Claire said.

***

Terry was sweating by the time he reached court three.

"All right, let's start simple," Claire said. "Just tap the ball back to me. Focus on control, not power."

Terry adjusted his sunglasses, gripped the paddle like a frying pan, and whacked the ball directly into the net.

"Hold the paddle like you're shaking someone's hand," Claire said.

Three more balls rolled around by the base of the net.

Claire flinched slightly but stayed upbeat. "Okay, let's try again."

This time, the ball launched over to court two and caught Ben in the back of his neck.

"JESUS!" Ben shouted, dropping his paddle.

"Relax, brother," Terry said. "It's not like it's a baseball."

"Yeah, well how about I hit one at you when you're not ready."

Terry's jaw tightened. "I'd love to see you try."

"All right, boys, let's focus," Claire said. "Terry, I want you to only focus on me and hit the ball softly back in my direction."

Two more balls into the net. And on the third, Terry tripped over his own boot and landed on his elbow.

Claire walked toward him. "You okay?"

Terry sat up slowly. "No, I'm not okay. I'm fifty-six years old with two bum knees and a foot that clicks when I fart."

Danny stepped in.

"Terry—"

"Don't patronize me, DeMarco."

He pointed at the others, voice booming. "This ain't my scene. I don't belong here. These people—what, they knit between games? Y'all got lemon water and matching visors like this is some retirement fantasy I forgot to buy into."

No one spoke. Terry kicked his paddle and turned toward the exit.

Danny stepped in fast, cutting him off at the gate.

Terry froze.

"You remember Hartford?" Danny asked. "I suplexed you off the top rope through that merch table. You popped up, hit me with a surfboard, and the crowd lost their minds."

Terry almost smiled. "You broke a rib, right?"

"Four."

They stood there, a moment of silence between them. Two battered men with thousands of bumps behind them—and no clear map ahead.

Danny kept his voice low. "You ruled the ring, man. No one's forgetting that."

Terry looked away.

"But the lights don't stay on forever," Danny continued. "And when they dim, it gets quiet. Lonely. You wake up sore and there's no curtain to walk through, no crowd to tell you who you are."

Terry didn't argue.

"But here? You get to write a new chapter. It's not the main event. But it's real. And yeah—you belong here, too."

From the court, Claire called out, "C'mon, Terry. We're all secretly hoping you peg Ben in the neck again."

A few players laughed.

Terry looked down at his boots. Then at Danny. "Fine," he muttered. "But I want one of those sweatbands. And next time I'm wearing sneakers."

***

It was just after 8:00 a.m. when Danny finally returned Jane's call.

"Is this a ghost or a miracle?"

"Depends who you ask," Danny said. "How are things?"

"Deadline's today. You in or out?"

Danny stared out the window. The early Florida sun streaked across the court outside. Terry was already there, sitting on the bench, taping up his ankle the same way he used to lace his boots.

"I'm in," Danny said. "But I've got conditions."

Jane exhaled like she'd been holding her breath for a week. "Talk to me."

"I want the deal as is. Appearances, salary, medical. But I want a company-sponsored initiative."

"Go on."

"The old-timers get to come to a series of pickleball clinics I'll run—then we hold a small annual tournament. Crowd, sponsors, the whole deal."

Jane paused.

"I'm serious," Danny said. "Keep the old guys active. Get them together. Let 'em compete without taking bumps. Let 'em feel like part of something again."

"You want a pickleball league," Jane said slowly.

"Exactly."

"That's actually...good. I'll talk to Sal. He'll love it if it means press without lawsuits."

She paused again, then added, "Congrats, Danny. You're officially old."

"I've been officially old since 2016," Danny said. "But thanks."

They hung up and Danny jogged toward the courts.

***

The Overbrook courts had never seen this many lawn chairs.

Claire cashed in another favor and had coordinated with the village to close off two extra blocks for parking.

A food truck with the word *Slamwiches* spray-painted across it was parked near the entrance. A woman sold sports drinks and shirts that read: LEGENDS DON'T DISAPPEAR. THEY RALLY.

Danny bought one.

There were no turnbuckles. No glamorous entrances. Just six courts, a folding table with a clipboard, and a line-up of busted knees, bad backs, and once-famous names now scribbled on round-robin brackets.

Danny stood near court one, clipboard in hand, watching Terry Tides serve underhand to a guy in a knee brace who once sold out an arena in Tokyo.

"You seeing this?" Claire asked. "You did this."

Danny didn't say anything right away. He scanned the courts. Ben laughing so hard he had to hold on to the net, William arguing calls like it was Wimbledon, a retired tag team (the Missing Socks) in matching compression sleeves slapping paddles and bumping bodies after every point.

He could still feel the crowd in his bones sometimes. That wild electricity when twenty thousand people chanted your name. He missed it more than he'd admit.

But this?

This was quiet. Human. Nice.

"It's funny," Danny said. "I used to think the crowd made you real. That if nobody popped, you didn't matter."

"And now?" Claire asked.

Danny shrugged. "Now I think the pop's overrated. This...this feels better. No character. No storyline. Just sweat and sun and people showing up."

Claire smiled and handed him a pickleball. "You ready?"

Danny looked at the court. Across the net, Rich Britchard stood in a bucket hat and a fanny pack, stretching like he hadn't played a sport in a decade.

"You're kidding," Danny said.

Rich pointed his paddle across the net like a sword. "You ready, Deadpan? Or will you need to fake an injury to avoid taking the loss?"

Danny smirked. "Don't tempt me. I've still got four Laugh Locks left in the chamber."

A few people chuckled. Someone yelled, "Do the laugh!"

He didn't. Not right away.

He walked to the baseline, bounced the ball once, and looked around at the small crowd. Some of them knew him from the old days. Most didn't.

Didn't matter.

He looked back at Rich.

Then he let it out.

"HAHAHAHAHAHA."

It wasn't for the crowd this time.

It was for him.

CROSSING PATHS: AN INTERVIEW WITH LILY O'CONNELL

Setting: A suburban intersection at 7:45 a.m. on a Tuesday. School zone signs flash yellow. Cars idle in a long line, exhaust visible in the cool morning air. LILY adjusts her bright yellow safety vest and checks her watch.

Intro: Every weekday morning and afternoon, roughly 2.8 million crossing guards take their posts at intersections across America. Most are retirees, part-time workers, or parents earning supplemental income. The job pays minimum wage in most districts, requires no special training beyond a brief safety course, and offers no benefits. Yet for many communities, the crossing guard represents something more than traffic control—a human presence in an increasingly automated world. Lily has been stationed at the corner of Maytag Road and Elm Street for twelve years, watching children grow up, seasons change, and neighborhoods evolve. In a role that others might see as simple or temporary, she has found both purpose and complexity.

Q: How have things changed through the years?

A: The stores on the corner flip over. The kids cycle in and out. But the intersection is the constant. Might be more cars and higher speeds, but it's simple: look left, look right, look left, and proceed with caution.

You have your parents that greet you with a big smile and a good morning. And the ones that pretend you're not standing there right next to them. The kids bring the smiles, though I usually gotta fish them out. Every year the kids seem to get quieter and quieter.

Q: What do you make of that—the kids getting quieter?

A: (Pause, adjusts her position.) Well, they're all looking down at their phones now. Even the little ones. Used to be they'd wave, ask questions, tell me about their pets or their weekend. Now they walk past like I'm...like I'm part of the scenery.

(Looks thoughtful.) Sometimes I wonder if I'm becoming invisible. Not just to the kids, but to everyone. Stand in the same spot long enough, maybe you just blend into the background. But then I think—maybe that's not such a bad thing. Maybe invisible people see more than anyone else.

Q: How do you handle the changing elements?

A: There have been mornings where I sit in the car to stay warm. One time, a parent called it in. When I see a kid or even an adult, I will always exit the vehicle to assist. But why would I stand there in the harshest of conditions when there's not a pedestrian in sight? Overall, it comes with turf. Just like the mailman, my job doesn't stop when the weather takes a turn.

Q: Someone actually called to complain about you staying warm in your car?

A: (Sighs.) Yeah. Apparently I wasn't "visible enough" to make them feel safe. Like I'm supposed to be a scarecrow out there, just for show. The thing is, I've been doing this for twelve years. I know when kids are coming, what time the buses run, when the crossing gets busy. But some parent sees me sitting in my car for five minutes and suddenly I'm not doing my job.

(Voice gets a little sharper.) That same parent probably never even looks up from their phone when they drop their kid off. But they've got time to call the school about me? It stung, I'll be honest. Made me question if I'm doing something wrong. But then I realized—I know this corner better than anyone. I know my job.

Q: Are there any tools of the trade?

A: The whistle has gone by the wayside. It's optional now, and you have to buy your own. The yellow rain slicker is a must. Good shoes. Dry socks. That's the key.

The socks. Cotton and wool blend in the winter. All cotton the rest of the year. I actually keep a spare pair in the glove box. Rarely need them. But it's the difference between comfort and discomfort. Health or the flu. The right socks, they're like a little hug for your feet.

Q: You're very specific about the socks. How'd you learn that?

A: (Chuckles.) Trial and error. Lots of error. My first winter, I thought any socks would do. By February, I was getting sick every other week. Harold—that's my husband—he said, "Lily, you can't take care of those kids if you can't take care of yourself."

It sounds silly, but having the right socks, the spare pair...it makes me feel prepared. Professional. Like I've thought through every possibility. When parents see me out there, I want them to know their kids are in good hands. Even if it's just about socks.

Q: Ever had a moment that shocked or scared you?

A: There've been a few over the years. Trucks flying through red lights like there's a checkered flag waving them home. But one time—maybe ten, twelve years ago—there was a kid. Jimmy Li. I can still see his face, clear as day.

His hat blew off, tumbled into the street. And he chased it. Fast. The car coming down didn't see him at first. Swerved just in time. Set off a chain reaction. Three-car fender bender, right there on Maytag Road.

ALL STORIES BY DREW G. ROSEN

Can you imagine that? A multicar accident on our sleepy little corner?

Now Jimmy drives by in a red Toyota. Waves every time he passes through.

Q: How did that change you?

A: (Long pause, looks down at her hands.) For weeks after, I couldn't sleep. Kept replaying it, thinking about what could've happened. What should've happened. Harold said I was being too hard on myself, but...that's a child. Someone's baby.

I started paying attention differently after that. Not just watching for cars and kids, but watching for...chaos, I guess. The unexpected. Wind direction. Ice patches. Which kids are the runners, which ones listen. It's like I developed eyes in the back of my head.

(Voice gets quieter.) Sometimes I wonder if I care too much. If I've made this job bigger than it needs to be. But then I see Jimmy wave, and I think: Maybe caring too much is better than not caring enough.

Q: Do you ever feel like this job is beneath you? Or that people don't take it seriously?

A: (Bristles slightly.) Beneath me? No. But do people take it seriously? (Shakes head.) Most folks think anyone can do this. "Just help kids cross the street, how hard can it be?"

But it's not just about the crossing. I know which kids are having trouble at home because they're quieter than usual. I know which parents are going through divorces because drop-off patterns change. I know when someone's lost a job because suddenly they're walking instead of driving.

(Pause.) Maybe that makes me nosy. But I prefer to think it makes me...aware. Caring. These kids, they're not just faces to me. They're people I'm responsible for, even if it's just for thirty seconds at a time.

Q: What do you think about between crossings?

A: Just normal stuff, I guess. What I'm going to make Harold for dinner. When Sharon, my daughter, will call. Christmas gifts for the grandkids and when I'll have time to get to the store. I try to avoid anything heavy like health and wealth. Those are rabbit holes that can turn a sunny day gray real fast. Like, what's the point? When I'm standing here on this corner there's not much I can do. There's no changing anything. No going back in time. No living for tomorrow. It's a job that takes awareness and being present in the here and now.

Q: But do you ever think about bigger things? What this all means?

A: (Looks out at the intersection.) You mean like, what's the point of it all? (Smiles sadly.) Sometimes. Especially on the quiet days, or when I'm sitting in the car trying to stay warm.

I think about how I've watched these kids grow up, move away, have kids of their own. And I'm still here, at the same corner. Sometimes that feels important—like I'm the constant in their changing world. Other times it feels...small. Like I'm just marking time. You know, I probably shouldn't share this, but (gets quiet) I name the animals. The birds. The squirrels. You'd be surprised how routine-oriented they can be. It sounds crazy, I know. What does any of it really mean?

(Pause.) But then I remember Jimmy Li. And I think maybe small things matter more than we know. Maybe keeping people safe for thirty seconds at a time is enough. Maybe it has to be.

Q: Ever think about retiring?

A: Harold's been mentioning it more lately. "Lily, you've done your part. Let someone else worry about those kids." But the thing is...who? They'd probably hire some teenager who doesn't know the patterns, doesn't know the kids' names, doesn't understand that this corner has its own personality.

(Voice gets uncertain.) Or maybe that's just my ego talking. Maybe anyone could do this job just fine, and I've convinced myself I'm irreplaceable because it makes me feel important.

I don't know. Some days I think I'll do this forever. Other days I wonder if I'm just scared to stop being needed.

FEEDING THE SILENCE

My dog died, so I started feeding the birds.

It began with a long plastic green tube filled with seeds hanging from a rusty metal hook in our tiny garden.

Once a day turned into three, which led to me hunching over my laptop with six browser tabs open, researching bird cams as cold April rain drummed on the roof. There's even one that promises AI technology smart enough to identify even the rarest of aviary wonders.

I tried to find bits and pieces of my four-legged bestie in each winged visit, but quickly learned that there was no message, no sign. The birds were just hungry.

The cardinals always come first. Followed by small brown wrens. The light gray mourning doves tend to make a late-afternoon visit—while the majestic blue jays are as unpredictable as the squirrels that regularly crash the feeding frenzy.

Now that Lincoln is gone, there are words and tears and birds—but in the end, there is nothing. Just memories that masquerade as reality, barely filling the void.

Every moment that used to belong to Lincoln—mornings, evenings, walks, mealtimes—now echoes with silence, replaced by the flutter of wings and indistinguishable chirps.

Lincoln, aka Love Puff, aka Blackie, aka Velveteen Dream, aka FishMouth, aka SnuggleCrow was mine and Sara's long before Kaitlyn and Ashley were born.

He was listed as a boxador—a boxer and Labrador mix—though Miss Nees, the shelter owner, told us that identifying his breed was a guessing game. It didn't matter to us.

His black fur glistened in the sunlight as we signed the paperwork and the way his ears flopped over his face made us forget about the five references we needed to provide. We had at first whined at the tediousness of the whole process, but after meeting Lincoln, we would have provided seven references if needed.

Lincoln was known as Giblets at the time (we never asked why) and had brown eyes that burrowed into your soul. We couldn't wait to bring this mutt back to our house to make it a home.

Our ability to keep him alive, especially during those first few weeks, validated our hypothesis that two people with full hearts and decent brains could care for living things beyond green plants, which, frankly, we were never great at to begin with. But with Lincoln, we thrived.

Training duties and daily walks became my responsibilities. Cleanups and feedings were taken on by Sara.

We both relished our new duties—neither of us saying what we both knew: it was our unspoken trial run to be parents, and we took every opportunity to spoil our new addition.

I ran home each day during lunch, a short but maddening stoplight-ridden drive, to let Lincoln stretch his legs outside and do his business. My brother Lou told me it was overkill, but only I saw how Lincoln's puppy posture changed when the tires crunched over the driveway gravel. And without fail, when I walked through the door, Lincoln's greeting made my life complete—every time, like the first time.

In those early months, a day couldn't pass without Sara ordering a bone, a toy, a supplement, an outfit, or just a good old-fashioned tennis ball for our boy.

It didn't take long for Lincoln to become my conversational companion. I knew he didn't understand, but that didn't stop me from sharing my joys, my annoyances, and my fears. For his sake, I hope those thick velvet curtain ears protected him from my woes: complaints about fertility, money problems, a job devoid of color—the poor pup received it all, his tail always wagging.

I chased off a squirrel today, banging a broom against the window. That used to be Lincoln's job—one he handled with more grace than I can muster.

Sara says I'm trying too hard with the birds—that I'm looking for something that isn't there. I remind her that the living room doesn't need to be vacuumed...again.

Grief hangs heavily but quietly. It splits us into separate parts of the house so that we may cope in our own way, not one voice raised. Instead, I stare at the yard and wait for birds to come and go. Sara sweeps the floors. We know that neither one of us is wrong.

When Kaitlyn was born, Lincoln had spent his entire life as the center of our universe. We worried he'd be jealous or confused, or worse—resentful. But he took to her instantly, curling up beside the Pack 'n Play like it was his duty. He sniffed her head once, sneezed, and looked at me like, *Okay, I'll keep watch.*

Through the 2:00 a.m. feedings and the 6:00 a.m. arguments about formula and finances, Lincoln stayed curled up at our feet. Though he couldn't fix anything, his presence alone made it all feel survivable.

By the time Ashley came along, Lincoln's face had gone salt-and-pepper, and his joints clicked when he stood up, but he still got himself to the door every morning to see the girls off to school. That was the thing about Lincoln: even when it hurt, he showed up.

The last couple of years were kind and cruel, an opportunity to be grateful for every minute together while watching the inevitable unfold. Long walks through the neighborhood became shorter, eventually shrinking to tiny victories for just getting outside. The fleeting gazes of pity from neighbors hit like bullets.

I pre-mourned like it was my job, trying to pay the pain in advance—as if borrowing tomorrow's tears could soften the blow.

Finally, it happened. One day I came home and found Lincoln in the wrong corner in the wrong room lying the wrong way—and I knew he was telling me it was the right time.

As Lincoln slipped away, the emptiness slipped in, even as the vet did her best to make the process gentle for us all. My blur of tears was dark, deep, and definitive.

I installed a new bird feeder last week. It's sturdier, harder for the squirrels to tip, and my feathered friends seem to like it. Robins and sparrows and red-winged blackbirds have joined the fray as if they've learned about the upgrade.

I watch them from the window and talk to them. Not because they understand—but because there are some words I still need to say out loud.

STUCK NO MORE: AN INTERVIEW WITH HAROLD LEEL

Setting: Seltip Ballpark rises from a sea of suburban parking lots, its brick facade and emerald field offering a welcome break from the beige monotony of office parks and chain restaurants. The stadium's hand-operated scoreboard clicks and whirs above weathered bleachers, while the smell of grilled onions drifts up from the concourse below. On game nights, tens of thousands of voices echo off the concrete and steel, mixing with the crack of the bat and vendors' cries advertising cold beer.

Intro: HAROLD slumps over on his stool and presses the "3" button on the elevator panel. Third floor, home of the suites. Air-conditioned boxes where men in golf shirts drink beers out of glasses while a baseball game unfolds in the background. The retired sports journalist turned elevator operator gives his take on the ballpark.

Q: Sorry for the obvious question, but ever get stuck?

A: No, never. My brother is in IUEC [International Union of Elevator Constructors] and I have him here every few weeks to take a look. He gets to take in a game and I get peace of mind. And the Francks [team owners] are really good about upkeep on this place. I'm immune to the motion. Dare I say, addicted to the mindlessness of it all. For decades my brain ran hot, frazzled. Deadlines and timelines widening my internal fault lines until I was on the decline. Here, in this elevator car, I'm impervious to the world. People come in and people go out. forty-two seconds is as long as I need to spend with any one person, and I like it that way.

Q: May I ask what you did before this?

A: Sports writer. Worked at *America Now* for almost four decades. Then they shut the printing press, asked us to water down our journalism like a fountain soda with too much ice, and bought us out four months later when we tripped all over the technology. One week paid out for every year. So after a taste of peace on the lake with my brother Bill, I knew my corporate days were behind me. I was a door greeter at a large hardware store for a few months, but my knees sure didn't like all that standing. Here I get to sit most of the time. I sit. I think. I breathe. That's more than I used to get to do. Making up for lost time, I guess.

Q: Do you miss anything about your newspaper days?

A: Cigarettes. Coffee. Lillian, I guess. She was the receptionist. Kept all of the trains on the track. And kept Douglas Bowen, the nastiest editor I've ever encountered, off all our backs. I remember one time, it was late July. Yankees were playing the Mets. On the verge of getting swept. It happened to be the same night we were celebrating Annie's fortieth. It was like some ungodly score in the sixth inning. Like seventeen to two, Mets. So for the first time and only time in my career, I filed the story early. Lillian said she'd revise the story if anything crazy happened in the last few innings. Thankfully, nothing did. But the whole time Annie and I were oohing and aahing over the melt-away steak and hazy sunset, I was worried that the Yankees' bats would come alive and Bowen would chew me out. Saw some great moments back in those days. But was it worth the burning in my chest and steady diet of TUMS? Probably not. Annie deserved more of my attention. Everyone did.

Q: Still watch the games?

A: I do but I don't. I mostly pick up bits and pieces from the folks that ride with me. I know Reynolds kept his hit streak alive last night and that the Rockies are running away with the division. But it's nicer to watch from above the forest than from the weeds. When I was getting paid, I had an obligation to ingest every detail and make it digestible on the page. Now that it's optional, I mostly opt out.

Q: Worst elevator joke you've heard?

A: If I'm honest, this job has its ups and downs, but the humor is nonexistent.

Q: What do you think about in between floors?

A: Not much. That's the luxury of it. Sometimes it's what I want for dinner. Sometimes it's nothing. But the nothing's what I needed, I think. After all those years thinking in headlines and word counts, it's nice to let the sentence go unfinished.

Content Warning: The following story deals with sensitive subject matter including references to violence.

IS THIS REALISTIC ENOUGH FOR YOU?

Our seventh-grade English teacher told us that fiction must create a universe. A place that the reader enters and doesn't want to leave. Or can't escape.

So, I've decided that I'm sitting in a windowless, painted black room. The only light flickers from the screen of my phone, the only smell is maple bacon, the kind Mom sometimes makes for Jenny and me on Sunday mornings to bribe us to church.

Hey reader, do you want to leave yet?

I hope not because Mrs. Efross will probably give me a C, which would be hard to explain to my dad. He sells carpets in West Meadow, one town over from us. And while he's never said it out loud, I've always assumed he didn't attend college, but that never stops him from lecturing me about good grades and being "well-adjusted." Whatever that means.

Even though the room is dark, I can navigate it with ease. I find a half-filled bottle of tepid water and chug it down. Stepping around my gaming chair, I open the drawer built into the side of my oak bed frame and reach inside.

It's still there. The gun. It sits heavy in my hand and even in the darkness, my pointer finger lands flawlessly on the trigger. I let it linger there for a few seconds before placing the gun back in the orange shoebox my slippers came in.

I know what you're thinking. I'm not that kid. But if I tell you what I'm really planning, you'll stop reading, and I need you to stay.

If Mackie DeLau had more bullets, I would have bought them. But he didn't, so I am singularly focused.

I should take back that last sentence because I fully recognize that I'm being too deliberate with my words. Mrs. Efross would want me to "show and not tell," so let me try that again:

Mackie DeLau led me to a metal filing cabinet sitting in the back of his musty basement. He opened the bottom drawer. Inside was a dusty cigar box that held some weird curled-up receipt, an old calculator, and a single silver bullet with a copper tip. If he'd had more bullets, I would have bought 'em. But he didn't, so now I've got just one. Which is enough, I guess, since I've only got one plan.

I prefer the first version, but I guess this writing thing has some written and unwritten rules.

Anyways, back in my room, I'm lying flat on my back. I breathe the way Dr. Mike taught me—slow and steady—when it feels like something's crackling behind my eyes. The heavy tension in my arms is a familiar, unwelcome guest.

My mind wanders back to the cafeteria last week. It smelled like corn. It *always* smells like corn, even when the lunch ladies are serving green beans. I was at the Na-migos table, which is what they call the loner table. It was me; Polly, who plays the cello; Humberto, who doesn't speak a lick of English; and Claire Sanders, with the frizzy hair and freckles. Claire and I have teamed up on school projects for years. In math, two negatives make a positive. In real life? Two introverts don't cancel each other out—they just sit in silence.

While Claire and I played Minecraft on my phone, building a block version of the school, Aidan, Raj, and Luke walked over to me. I don't want to waste your time with descriptions, so imagine a quarterback, his wannabe shadow, and a short boy who gets away with everything because his dad once won a famous reality show.

Ugh, that was probably another part where I was supposed to show and not tell. Sorry, Mrs. Efross. But honestly, the readers know the exact boys I'm talking about.

"You going to the Burger Shack later?" Aidan asked me.

"Nah," I replied, keeping the focus on my phone.

"Why?" Raj asked. "Have a date with your left hand?"

Luke snorted way too hard and drew a dirty look from Claire.

"What are you looking at, Clair Stare?" Aidan asked. He obviously didn't want an answer, just the upper hand, so he could feel better about himself for a hot minute. To get everyone to chill, I knocked over my water bottle and the water streamed off the edge of the lunch table, pooling onto the attached bench.

"Nice job, Zesty," Aidan said as he and the boys walked away, each brushing me on the way by.

I laughed to show them they hadn't gotten to me. But my fingers were clenched so tight around my phone, I swear I heard something crack.

The clatter of the cafeteria blinks out, and I'm back on my bed, staring at a ceiling I can't see.

Dad yells up that dinner is ready. I reach over and grabb my phone, which is charging in the dark. One hundred percent battery and unread texts from Polly, Claire, and Jed. I flip the phone over so it faces down on the mattress.

So many people interpret the quiet and darkness as signs of weakness. A signal of failure. But they don't realize that Dickinson wrote, like, eighteen hundred poems in the dark. Billie Eilish recorded her best album with the shades pulled tight. I'm pretty sure Minecraft was coded mostly with the lights off, too. There's brilliance in the shadows.

"Sammy, dinner!" my dad yells, hoping a more forceful approach will get me downstairs to pretend we're a normal family.

"One minute," I reply.

I unzip my canvas school bag and return to the drawer under my bed. I open the shoebox cover and slide the

ALL STORIES BY DREW G. ROSEN

gun into the backpack's main compartment, under my math binder.

One shot. No do-over.

The house gets quiet for a minute like it's waiting on me.

Then comes the clink of forks and Jenny laughing too loud at one of dad's bad jokes.

I pull the blanket up over my head, even though it's hot. It dulls the sounds drifting up from downstairs. I feel far away, like I'm buried in something thick and dark, which I guess is what Mrs. Efross would call a simile.

I drift off into the deepest, richest sleep of my entire life. When I wake up at 4:00 a.m., I feel clear. Confirmed. Like my bag is packed with everything I needed.

A couple hours later, I get dressed like it's any other Tuesday. Black hoodie, black jeans, white socks from the laundry pile.

In the kitchen, Dad's talking about some big sale he's hoping to make today. Jenny is already halfway through a toaster waffle.

"Sleep okay?" Dad asks.

"Yeah," I say, which is technically true.

I pour some Froot Loops, sit down, and eat every bite.

I take my usual walk to school. The one that takes me behind the Pembroke Apartments and off the main road. The route takes a little longer but allows me to clear my mind. Avoiding noisy cars and disgusting exhaust fumes is a bonus. I pop my earbuds in and crank some Pantera to the max.

As I rejoin the main road, I bump into Claire walking with her head buried in her phone. She almost doesn't notice me.

"Oh, hey, Sam," she says. I see a flicker of excitement in her eyes that is quickly dulled by whatever pills her parents have been jamming down her throat.

I hold my hand up in acknowledgment.

"I stayed up late trying to get the gym roof to look like yours," she says. "I still don't know how you made that curved bleacher thing."

She lives for Minecraft. It's kind of tragic.

We enter the school at the same time. I go left for English class, and she goes right for math.

As I walk into Mrs. Efross's class, I pass Aidan and Raj, who are giggling about something.

I sit at my desk and unzip my school bag as it hangs off my left shoulder. I reach in and pull out:

a story.

This story.

I am going to hand it to Mrs. Efross now. And after she reads it, I'll wait until she looks up. I'm excited to see her face when she realizes this time, I really followed the assignment.

ABOUT THE AUTHOR

Drew G. Rosen writes fiction about the quiet digni-ty of everyday life and the unexpected connections that bind us. *Before the Sink Overflows* is his debut collec-tion, shaped during the quiet hours following the loss of his beloved Shiba Inu, Kenji. The time once spent walking together became space to reflect—and to write. He lives in New York with his wife and teenage son and is at work on a novel.

THE STORY CONTINUES—
COME READ WHAT'S NEXT

Thank you for spending time with *Before the Sink Over-flows (and Other Warning Signs of Hope)*.

If these stories rang true for you, I'd love to keep the conversation going.

I'm finishing a novel that digs even deeper into the small disasters and quiet triumphs we share.

Join my reader circle and I'll email you the opening pages.
You'll be the first to:

- Read the draft's first scenes (before anyone else)
- Vote on cover concepts
- Get launch-day bonuses reserved for early supporters

https://drewography.com/fiction/

One More Way to Help

A brief, honest review is the lighthouse that guides new readers to these stories.

If a particular piece pulled at your heart or made you think, would you share a few kind words in a review wherever you bought the book? It makes a world of difference.

Thank you for walking beside these characters—and me.

—Drew G. Rosen